JACK REACHER'S SPECIAL INVESTIGATORS (COMPLETE BOOKS #1, #2 & #3)

A USA TODAY BESTSELLING SERIES

DAN AMES

Slogan Books, New York, NY

A USA TODAY BESTSELLING BOOK

Book One in The JACK REACHER Cases

CLICK HERE TO BUY NOW

Free Books And More

Would you like a FREE copy of my story BULLET RIVER and the chance to win a free Kindle?

Then sign up for the DAN AMES BOOK CLUB:

For special offers and new releases, sign up here

… A USA TODAY BESTSELLING AUTHOR

DEAD MEN WALKING

SET IN THE REACHER UNIVERSE BY PERMISSION OF LEE CHILD

DAN AMES

Copyright © 2020 by Dan Ames

All rights reserved.

No part of this book may be reproduced in any form or by any electronic or mechanical means, including information storage and retrieval systems, without written permission from the author, except for the use of brief quotations in a book review.

Praise for Dan Ames

"Fast-paced, engaging, original."
>	New York TIMES BESTSELLING AUTHOR Thomas Perry

"Ames is a sensation among readers who love fast-paced thrillers."
>	MYSTERY TRIBUNE

"Cuts like a knife."
>	Savannah Morning News

"Furiously paced. Great action."
>	New York TIMES BESTSELLING AUTHOR Ben Lieberman

Free Books And More

**Would you like a FREE copy
of my story BULLET RIVER and the
chance
to win a free Kindle?**

**Then sign up for the DAN AMES BOOK
CLUB:**

For special offers and new releases, sign up here

Dead Men Walking

(Jack Reacher's Special Investigators)

Book One

by

Dan Ames

"There will be killing until the score is paid."

-Homer *THE ODYSSEY*

Chapter 1

He could smell her across the room.

Amid the various odors of stale beer, spilled liquor, cigarette smoke, pot, sweat, body odor, kitchen grease, perfume and cheap cologne, the scent seemed to linger in his senses. Tickling him, teasing him like a forgotten lover's tongue.

His eyes stared straight ahead, but the mirror behind the bar ran the length of the room and it was easy to spot her. He'd already noted the position of the air-conditioning vent and the way the thin layer of smoke near the ceiling was pushed in his direction. Its path swept directly over the head of the sandy-haired woman wearing skinny jeans, a tight black T-shirt and gold hoop earrings. Her hair was a shade darker than dishwater blonde and it was pulled back over her ears, held in place by a pair of black Ray-Ban sunglasses. She had a lean face, strong neck and a body that spoke of either fitness or organized athletics.

In any event, she'd come to his attention.

Or, at least, her aroma had.

It wasn't her perfume, or anything else superficial. No, what he could detect was something much more primal.

He drained the last of his beer, ordered another one and when the bartender placed it before him, he glanced over at the woman. She wasn't looking his way but he continued to stare until she caught his eye.

Her expression didn't change.

He could tell her eyes were blue, and they had widened in recognition of his interest, and her nostrils flared the tiniest fraction. They were microscopic nonverbal cues that he automatically interpreted. None of them was a surprise.

Her face was hiding any emotion, but physiologically, he could tell he was having an effect on her.

He looked away first.

Turned his attention back to the mirror and in its reflection, saw her turn back to her friends and say something.

The beer was cold and his finely tuned palate savored the slightly malty flavor of the hops. The alcohol had no effect on him whatsoever. While the blonde considered her reaction to his blatant challenge, he waited and studied himself in the mirror.

A good-looking man, no doubt. Not arrogance on his part, just an observation.

Long ago, he'd read about the ancient Romans and how they had distilled physical beauty into a numerical equation that represented an ideal spatial alignment. The brilliant minds of that time had been able to apply that formula to various aspects of the human body that the mind found pleasing.

His face would have qualified. All features fit into that spatial equation: the eyes just far enough apart, the size of the nose, the mouth and forehead. He was classically handsome, despite his size.

The rest of his body also met those requirements, but on a much larger scale. He was nearly six and a half feet tall and one heavy meal away from three hundred pounds. Yet his body fat would be the envy of an Olympic athlete for his frame was cloaked in muscle and not much else.

Something the blonde's friends failed to notice.

Three of them, all slightly bigger than normal but small compared to him, approached.

They stood behind him and waited for him to recognize their appearance.

He didn't.

He just drank from his beer and looked over at the blonde. She was staring at him. Her eyes were even wider, nostrils opened more, mouth slightly parted. He could smell her excitement, in addition to the pheromones that practically came off her in waves.

Behind him, the men bore the other scents; beer, smoke and from one of them, fear.

"Hey, dipshit," one of them said.

Since that wasn't his name, he didn't turn around.

One of them tapped his left shoulder.

The bartender made a beeline for the end of the bar where he was sitting. An older guy with a dirty T-shirt sporting a Corona beer logo. He held up his hands, one of which held a dirty dishrag.

"Now come on, Joe, he wasn't botherin' anyone."

The biggest of the trio who stood in the middle responded.

"Connie said he was staring at her," he said. "Making her feel downright uncomfortable."

He saw the man named Joe's reflection in the mirror. A big guy with a scruffy beard. Young, maybe just over twenty-one. His two buddies looked like him. One of them was fidgeting and he figured that was the guy who was scared.

"That true, mister?" the bartender asked.

"If Connie is the one with the tight jeans and nice ass, yes I most certainly was looking at her."

The hand that had tapped his shoulder now fell on it and pulled.

He turned and stood.

His height wasn't something they'd expected. He was now looking down on the three of them by at least four inches. Their body language spoke a combination of fear, anger and excitement.

"Outside right now or I call the cops," the bartender said.

The big man who'd just admitted he'd been staring at the trio's female friend led the way but when he was halfway across the barroom, he glanced over at Connie, raised a finger, and gestured for her to follow.

She did.

Outside, the cool Virginia air enlivened his senses even more. Instead of stopping just outside the door to the bar, he kept walking until he left the cone of light provided by the overhead sign and entered the shadows in the parking lot.

Only then did he turn.

It was as if he was watching a movie he'd seen many, many times. Somehow, he simply knew Joe was going to start to ask him a question and then step in and throw a punch before he finished.

It was an old trick so cliché the big man almost felt insulted that Joe had tried it on him.

"So where are you from—" Joe began and then his feet turned in preparation for the move he thought was going to be a strategic surprise. Maybe even a game-ender.

The punch was meant to be fast and powerful, sort of a cross between a right hook and a haymaker.

The big man watched it come and also saw Joe's buddies step forward. One more eagerly than the other.

He leaned back, let Joe's fist flash by his face and then he stepped in, hooked Joe's forearm with his left, brought up his right, and trapped it. It was then incredibly easy to apply opposite pressure.

Joe's arm literally snapped in two, held together only by the skimpiest shred of skin and ligament. The sound was quite loud in the still night air and the silence of the parking lot. Joe sagged and fell backwards.

The braver of the other two continued forward and threw a punch that had no hope of causing any damage. It had some power, but not enough, and it was launched without a good angle. It came toward the big man way too high and way too slow, like a bad decision one was forced to live with.

The big man, who'd partially turned in order to break Joe's arm, simply continued his pivot and lashed out with his right leg, performing a sweep that knocked Joe's first defender off his feet.

The attacker landed on his back in a heap. When he tried to get up, a fist crashed into his face, breaking his teeth, nose, jaw and skull in one shot. The fracture of the skull was only a hairline break, but the damage to his face was severe. It was as if the big man's fist had hit a plastic face and the flimsy material simply sagged inward.

Only one of Joe's crew remained, the one from which the unmistakable scent of fear emanated.

And then there was Connie.

The big man glanced at her, which turned out to be a mistake because he had assumed the coward would run. Instead, Joe's last buddy still in the game pulled out a switchblade knife and drove it into the big man's side.

"Yeah," Joe growled, from the ground.

The big man caught the coward's wrist, gave it a twist and heard bones crack. He then grabbed the knife by the handle and pulled it from his body. He looked at the blood on the blade with curiosity.

Still holding the knife wielder, he pulled him close, lay the knife against his throat and pressed, then drove the blade in and away. It tore through the man's throat, scraped against vertebrae. A huge, ugly gash opened and a river of blood poured down the man's chest. He sagged and the big man pushed him away. His now lifeless body landed on the gravel of the parking lot.

Connie screamed.

The big man turned and stepped over to Joe's other buddy whose face was caved in. The man was choking on blood and his body convulsing.

The man put the tip of the knife above the fallen man's heart and drove it in. The choking man gave one last cataclysmic spasm and he too, died.

Joe was next.

Connie was slowly backing away.

"Look, we were just—" she started to say.

The big man raised the knife and his mind ran a series of calculations involving the quality of the blade, its length, the amount of force needed, and the unique construction of the human skull.

He twisted and drove his arm down with incredible speed. The force of it drove the knife through Joe's hair, pierced his cranium and macerated his brain tissue. The big man twisted the knife and he heard Connie scream again, this one more terror-filled than the last.

The big man straightened up, walked to her and reveled in her scent. Her pheromones were even stronger than before. There was fear, yes. Revulsion, certainly. But there was eagerness.

Excitement. And sexual desire; the same desire he'd first smelled in the bar.

His enormous hand closed over her wrist and he pulled her toward his vehicle.

Later, in his hotel room, he calmly removed her clothes and then disrobed himself.

"Are you serious?" she asked, her voice hollow. She was pale and dazed. He knew she was in shock. "You were just stabbed."

Strangely, his shirt was bloody, but she couldn't see the stab wound on his body.

Her eyes went to a tattoo across his chest.

ACE.

He grabbed her by the throat and spread her legs apart.

"Oh, I'm done bleeding. But honey, you're just getting started."

Chapter 2

Frances Neagley prepared to leave her office. It was a somewhat early departure for her as she was usually the last to leave the building, often staying several hours after most had begun to take leave beginning at five o'clock or so.

Today was different.

As one of the founding members of Pinnacle Security, one of the largest private investigative firms in Chicago, she occupied a corner office on the top floor of a high-rise in the Loop. Her desk was always immaculate and today was no exception. In fact, her entire office was spotless with zero clutter. Across from her desk were two visitor chairs and behind them off to the side was a more relaxed sitting area with a coffee table, couch and two more chairs.

To the right, along the wall was a bank of

windows and a side table that was used for coffee, drinks or other refreshments if she was welcoming clients.

There was not a single personal item on display in her office. No family photos. No keepsakes. Nothing that reflected who Frances Neagley was as a person outside her position at Pinnacle.

She walked out of her office, nodded at her assistant, a young man named David who'd graduated from Northwestern with a degree in criminal justice, and took the elevator to the executive parking garage. There, she unlocked her BMW 7 Series and fired up the V12 engine.

Neagley expertly maneuvered the car out of the lot, and was soon heading north along the lakeshore to her home in Lake Forest.

But she wasn't going straight home.

Which is why she'd left the office earlier than normal.

She drove fast, relishing the power of the BMW's engine and a few minutes before reaching the outskirts of Lake Forest, she turned onto a side road and followed it to a small cluster of buildings not far from the railroad tracks.

There was a large structure clad in aluminum siding separate from the other buildings. Above the set of blue double doors that marked the business entrance was a sign: Lake Forest Animal Shelter.

Neagley parked in a lot across the street from the shelter, pushed the start/stop button on the BMW and the engine fell silent.

She sat and watched the building. It was cool outside with a slight chill in the air and the leaves on the trees on the other side of the railroad tracks were still green. In a matter of weeks they would begin to change color as fall arrived.

It was Neagley's favorite time of year.

The doors to the shelter opened and a woman stepped out. She had three dogs on leashes and walked them around to the back of the building.

Neagley was glad the woman hadn't glanced over to where she was parked. She'd been coming to the shelter every week or so, without ever going inside.

The thing of it was, Frances Neagley had been alone nearly all of her life. Her childhood had been something she'd worked to forget and eventually she had succeeded in banishing it from her daily thoughts.

She'd joined the Army to escape home, and landed in the 110th MP where she met her mentor, Jack Reacher. Since leaving the military Neagley had worked with Reacher several times, including one horrible case involving several members of the 110th who'd been murdered.

That had been some time ago, however, and

since then, Neagley had not heard from any of the people she'd known in the military.

She lived for her work and had often been told that she was the very best at what she did.

True or not, Neagley was a force of nature, and she knew how to get things done.

So the indecisiveness she now felt was a foreign feeling to her.

The fact she was trying not to admit was that for the first time in her life, she perhaps felt a touch lonely. Her career was everything to her. Neagley had a passion for investigation, and helping bring about justice in the world. As a young girl, no one had been there to do the same for her.

She'd been toying around with adopting a dog from the shelter. Neagley had always loved animals and far back in the memories she'd banished from her consciousness was a dog. She wasn't sure of the breed or the name and it really didn't matter anyway.

Inside that building was a dog she could adopt and eventually bring home with her.

It was a huge step.

For several moments she sat, drumming her fingers along the top of the steering wheel. Eventually, she realized it was a step that she just wasn't willing to take.

At least not today.

She fired up the BMW and put the big car into gear.

Minutes later, she pressed the button to her automatic gate and rolled the car through the entrance to her home. A long winding driveway led to her house, a stone and timber structure built in the 1920s. Five bedrooms. Six bathrooms. A home gym. Sauna. And pool. With spectacular views of Lake Michigan.

Corporate life had been very good to Frances Neagley, especially once she'd obtained partial ownership of the firm. That development had helped everyone involved.

She stopped at the mailbox, retrieved the day's collection and pulled the BMW into the four-car garage. The door shut automatically behind her.

Inside, Neagley walked to the door leading to the house, paused and pressed her thumb against a pad. A green light appeared signifying the door's alarm had been deactivated. She opened the door, stepped inside and entered the full alarm system's code on the keypad, shutting off the motion detectors.

Neagley walked through a mudroom and entered a hallway, turning left into the kitchen.

It was a space that would make a gourmet chef drool and Neagley hardly ever used it. She didn't cook much because, frankly, she didn't eat much either.

She set her keys into an antique arts and crafts bowl and set the mail down on the granite countertop.

Her eyes went to a single postcard.

It was blank on the front.

On the back it said, "Hope you can join us for our Halloween Eve holiday party. No RSVP required."

Neagley frowned, turned it over.

There was no return address.

She was about to throw it into the trash when something gave her pause.

Neagley checked the postmark: New York City.

There was only one person she knew who lived in New York. A fellow member of the 110th MP.

Karla Dixon.

And then, suddenly, she knew.

Halloween Eve.

October 30th.

10/30.

1030.

Army code.

It stood for: *military policeman in urgent need of assistance*.

Karla Dixon was in trouble.

Chapter 3

There was no question the act was futile; Neagley did it anyway. She thumbed through the contact list on her phone, found Dixon and dialed the number.

It went straight to voicemail. She left a message asking Dixon to call her.

If Dixon had her phone and was able to make or receive calls, she wouldn't have sent the odd message to Neagley using a subtle reference to 1030. But Neagley made the call just to be able to cross it off her list. It was the first thing anyone would do.

The strange postcard could mean only one thing: Dixon was either under tight surveillance or worse. Neagley didn't have to consider the extreme options as she was all too familiar with what the world could do to women.

Dead Men Walking (Jack Reacher's Special Investigators)

As one of Jack Reacher's Special Investigators in the Army, Neagley had seen and done it all. Especially crimes against women. As a male-dominated organization, women were a minority and more often the victims of violent crime.

Pretty much every kind of case had passed across her desk in a case file. The Special Investigators had been very good at what they did. They even had coined their own slogan: *You do not mess with the Special Investigators.*

Related to that was a second, more unofficial theme: if you mess with the Special Investigators, you are dead men walking.

Panic was not in Neagley's vocabulary.

She set her briefcase on the kitchen counter, asked her high-end coffee machine to make her an espresso and while she waited, thought about Dixon.

Karla Dixon had always been a key member of the Special Investigators. Small, dark-haired and with a blazing intellect, she had a passion for numbers. Dixon and Reacher would spend hours discussing prime numbers, sequential combinations, mathematical theories and numerical oddities.

It was what had bound them together, and Neagley suspected, eventually led them to form a romantic relationship once they'd both left the military. It had happened, she had always assumed, during the investigation of the murders of four of the Special Investigators: Tony Swan, Manuel Orozco, Calvin Franz and Jorge Sanchez.

When they'd worked together to track down their killers, Neagley was pretty sure Reacher and Dixon had taken their relationship to the next level. Reacher wouldn't have allowed that to happen when they were still in the Army and she was under his command. Reacher wasn't that kind of guy.

But once they were free of that dynamic, Neagley was pretty sure it happened.

It didn't matter to her, one way or the other.

What did matter was that Dixon had reached out to her with an urgent request for assistance and Neagley needed to figure out why.

Her espresso machine let out a long hiss of steam and she went over and grabbed the small, delicate cup, and sipped the hot beverage. It was rich and strong, she wouldn't drink all of it or she'd be up all night.

The Special Investigators had practically lived on coffee back in the day. It was one of Reacher's basic food groups.

Now, Neagley retrieved her laptop, set it on the counter, and looked up Dixon's email. She sent a brief message, asking Dixon to contact her.

Again, she knew it was a futile act. If Dixon had been able to send and receive email, the mysterious 1030 message never would have been needed. Neagley was simply doing what anyone would do; reach out via the normal channels.

She was just crossing the obvious things off the list.

It was necessary because Neagley had already asked herself one very important question: *if someone was watching Dixon, how did she know they weren't watching her, too?*

Chapter 4

The surveillance was quite simple.

With the continued power supplied by the controversial Patriot Act, monitoring a civilian's communications required very little effort. Once a certain protocol was followed, and the necessary approvals were signed off on, it was a matter of assigning a technical team to identify the appropriate channels (i.e., cell phones, email, computer apps, etc.) and establish access. After that, actual eyes were required to review the content supplied by the technical team.

In this case, the agent was a man seated in front of a computer terminal, scanning streams of text.

He was in a nondescript building not far from the nation's capitol. He wore no identifying tags or badges, the office itself bore no corporate name or logo and when asked what he did for a living, he simply replied he worked in data entry.

Which was one hundred percent true.

When the messages appeared on devices belonging to one Dixon, Karla, the agent noted the sender: Neagley, Frances.

The man highlighted the content and included the sender's name. He also attached all government records belonging to Neagley, Frances.

Once bundled, the entire batch of data was sent "upstream" where the agent had little doubt it would be received and reviewed immediately.

Chapter 5

The espresso kicked in and Neagley felt the surge in her veins. She wasn't tired; she rarely felt fatigue and only slept a handful of hours every night. Ordinarily, she would probably hit her home gym and put in a good two hours of exercise: running on the treadmill, lifting weights, and punching the heavy bag.

But not tonight.

Instead, she went upstairs, changed out of her business suit and put on jeans, a black T-shirt and running shoes. Back downstairs, she grabbed her purse and keys, went out to the garage, and fired up the BMW. There were some things she could have done at home in terms of looking into Dixon's whereabouts but going back into her office would give her plenty more resources. It would also give her the luxury to conduct some cyber investigation behind a much more robust firewall than the one she had in her private home. Her security firm was a veritable fortress, kept up to date with the latest and greatest technology available anywhere in the world.

Traffic was light as she put the big V12 engine to good use. She nearly cut the time it had taken her to get home in half and soon she was parking in her assigned space. Neagley took the executive elevator up to her office and noted there were still a few people working. No one paid her attention; they were used to seeing her in the office at all hours of the day and night.

On her desk was a slim computer linked to the company's security network. As one of the principals of the firm, Neagley knew exactly how much money had been invested in the latest tools available to private investigators like herself and her team. The equipment – both hardware and software - had been well in the six-figure range, nearing the seven-figure.

Additionally, they'd invested in the absolute best cloaking services, to prevent any trackbacks to the firm's forays into digital snooping.

It was another reason Neagley had opted to perform her Dixon searches at the office – if someone actually was watching and/or monitoring it would be much more difficult, if not impossible, to trace it back to Neagley.

To begin, Neagley used her access to a private Army database for which she paid no small annual fee, and there was able to gather Karla Dixon's private information, including her social security number as well as her last known address.

Next, Neagley booted up a program the firm called TRACKER. It was a proprietary blend of several systems, heavily encrypted to hide both the originating source and the target databases. Cloaking was done by another system the legality of which was somewhat dubious. Neagley had entered the information she had gathered for Karla Dixon from the military database, as well as what she'd already had in her contact information.

Then, she turned TRACKER loose.

While the complex program worked its magic, Neagley thought about another one of the team members of the Special Investigators: Edgar Chavez. Back in the day, he'd always been one of the team's best investigators. He had a fine attention to detail and a very high IQ. Whenever a program had become highly complicated, it always seemed Chavez had been the one to break it down into its simplest components. Back then, computers were a relatively new thing, so Chavez hadn't been able to apply his considerable intellect in their direction.

But since then, Chavez, like the rest of them, had all left the Army and gone into private practice. Neagley had kept tabs on all of them and knew that Chavez had done a deep dive into cyber security and eventually, made it the primary focus of his own firm down in Venice, Florida.

She thought of Chavez because if TRACKER didn't come up with enough information, she knew Edgar could. Especially when it came to someone like Dixon. They all loved her, and Chavez was no exception.

Neagley wanted to wait. No need to ring a false alarm and jump the gun.

It was too early to bring in any of the other Special Investigators. She would forge ahead, on her own, and only contact them if necessary.

Just as she came to that conclusion, TRACKER began to spit out information.

Neagley watched as the results appeared on her screen, almost like entries in a journal.

There were past addresses. Initially, after she'd left the Army, Dixon had lived in Washington, DC. After that, she'd gone to New York and there were several addresses listed, separated by several years each. The last address matched the one Neagley had on her phone under Dixon's contact information.

Next came Dixon's tax returns.

Neagley let out a low whistle. Karla Dixon had done very well for herself. There were two employment records that showed Dixon had worked for two different financial institutions, in their corporate security departments.

Finally, Dixon had landed in her last job, which she had held for over a dozen years and appeared to be a principal in the firm. It was called FT Investigations, based in Manhattan.

In many ways, Dixon's career path matched Neagley's own.

But then something caught Neagley's eye.

TRACKER was able to identify license plates. According to the DMV records, Dixon owned an Audi SUV with New York plates. The license plate was last seen nearly a week ago, leaving the city.

Neagley was able to ask TRACKER to look for any images from highway cameras.

One photo popped up on Neagley's screen.

It was an Audi SUV, with a license plate that matched Dixon's.

There was only one occupant of the vehicle.

Behind the wheel.

A man with dark sunglasses and a scarf covering half of his face.

It definitely was not Karla Dixon.

Neagley studied the image and exited TRACKER.

It was time to book a flight and get to the airport.

She was going to New York.

To find Karla Dixon.

Chapter 6

Guns.

One of the advantages of owning a large security firm with offices all over the world is the ease with which one can quickly acquire important resources.

Ordinarily, flying would create a problem of landing in a new destination sans any personal protection.

Not so for Frances Neagley.

One call to the New York office of Pinnacle Security was all it took. When she landed on the direct flight from O'Hare to LaGuardia she was met by a young associate in a black sedan. He handed her the keys to the car and popped the trunk for her.

When she placed her suitcase inside the trunk,

Neagley noted several military-grade cases she knew contained weapons.

The associate disappeared and Neagley got behind the wheel. She'd worked in New York many times and knew her way around. So without consulting a map or the navigation app on her phone, she pointed the car in the direction of Manhattan. After crossing the Queensboro Bridge and cruising alongside the East River, she made her way to Midtown. Once there, she entered the address of Dixon's employer into her navigation app and used it to direct her there.

FT Investigations, the name of Dixon's firm, was located inside a towering structure of steel and glass with an underground parking garage.

Perfect, Neagley thought.

She collected a ticket and drove to the lower level and found a parking space. She backed into it, leaving herself enough room behind the vehicle.

Neagley got out of the car, went to the trunk and opened it. With a quick glance to make sure no one was around and there were no security cameras, she opened one of the cases provided by her associate. A brand-new Glock 41 chambered in .45 Auto. It was Neagley's favorite gun not only because the .45 caliber was her ammo of choice, but because the Glock 41 carried 13 rounds.

She shrugged on a shoulder holster, fitted

underneath a blue blazer. With her jeans, T-shirt and black athletic shoes, Neagley looked like a hip young executive.

After locking the car, she rode the elevator to the main lobby and found a directory.

FT Investigations was located on the top floor.

Neagley rode the elevator up and the doors opened to reveal an expansive floor of white marble with a reception desk at the far end. She was immediately struck by how similar Dixon's firm was to her own back in Chicago.

She approached the front desk. A young man dressed in all black glanced up at her. He had a headset with a clear microphone that extended along his jawline and stopped an inch short of the corner of his mouth. He had a wisp of a moustache in sore need of additional testosterone.

"May I help you?" he asked.

"Yes, I'm Frances Neagley and I'm here to see Karla Dixon."

"I'm afraid she's out of the office right now," he responded. "May I take a message?"

Neagley noticed that he didn't even check a computer or desktop calendar.

"Do you know when she'll be back?"

This time he tapped on his keyboard, glanced at his screen and said, "It appears she's on vacation and I don't see a return date."

He looked up at Neagley with an expression of finality.

"I see, is that common at this firm? To go on vacation indefinitely?"

"I don't know, ma'am," he replied. "May I take a message?"

"No," she answered.

He gave her a curt nod, turned away and spoke into his headset. "Hello, FT Investigations, how may I help you?"

Neagley studied the glass door off to her right. She could see a row of offices and cubicles.

She crossed the lobby and got back into the elevator.

Neagley was neither surprised nor disappointed.

It's what she expected.

Now, she was going to head to Karla Dixon's apartment. There, she wasn't quite as sure what she might find.

Chapter 7

Although Neagley thought she and Dixon shared some similarities in terms of their workplace, any commonalities ended when she took a cab to Dixon's apartment. Neagley had decided to leave the car in the underground parking lot of the office in Midtown as Dixon's place wasn't far enough away to merit the hassle of looking for a parking space.

So, she had retrieved her overnight bag, left the rest of the guns in the car's trunk, and cabbed it over to Dixon's.

The address Neagley's research had turned up belonged to a luxury high-rise, not dissimilar from the building housing Dixon's place of work. It was steel and glass, with a doorman and a lobby that was hushed and smelled like vanilla and lilac.

Security was impressive, too.

Dead Men Walking (Jack Reacher's Special Investigators)

Neagley noted multiple cameras and even from across the lobby she spotted the key card reader next to the elevator.

She weighed her options as she walked forward with a purposeful stride. The doorman was off to her left and to the far right, a woman sat behind an elaborate French desk facing a computer. Above the elevator, she saw the lights changing and strode quickly for the doors.

The doors opened and an older couple emerged. They were dressed in matching exercise clothes and the man was adjusting a sports watch on his wrist. As they stepped off the elevator, the woman said, "Here we go, George!"

Neagley nodded and stepped aside to let them pass, then she ducked inside the open elevator. She was relieved there wasn't an additional security card reader on the inside in order to activate the buttons for floors.

Dixon lived on Floor 21. Neagley pushed the button.

She couldn't help but wonder if Dixon had purposely chosen that floor. Dixon was crazy about numbers, always had been. Neagley had spent many a long evening listening to Dixon and Reacher endlessly discussing prime numbers, factors, theories and other mathematical oddities.

The number 21 didn't mean anything to Neagley, other than it was the legal drinking age in most states and was the number of the star running back for the Chicago Bears.

None of which meant anything to Dixon, she was certain.

The elevator stopped and Neagley stepped out into an equally lush and quiet but smaller lobby from which two hallways diverged.

Neagley guessed and took the hallway to the right. Dixon's apartment number was 2110 which made her smile: the Army's 110th MP. A coincidence? Probably not.

The carpet was dark blue, the walls a silvery, textured wallpaper with modern art placed every twenty feet or so. She found herself facing Dixon's door and wondered about the security.

If Dixon had been expecting trouble, she would have certainly armed a security system, which she most likely had installed in her apartment. Like Neagley, Dixon had seen no small amount of crimes against women and that knowledge certainly would have inspired her to have a high-quality alarm system in her home.

However, if Dixon hadn't been the last person in her apartment – a distinct possibility as TRACKER had shown someone else driving Dixon's car – then the security system probably wasn't armed.

Thankfully, the modern apartment building had chosen to go traditional with the apartment doors and Neagley was facing a standard door handle and lock, along with a deadbolt.

Slipping a slim black case from a pocket inside her blazer, Neagley selected a pair of lock picks; one that finished in a straight point, another that featured a slight curve and hook.

Working quickly, knowing the hallway was probably being monitored, she was able to unlock the door and snap back the dead bolt in less than forty seconds.

She hoped it was fast enough.

Neagley stepped into Dixon's apartment and shut the door behind her. Her eyes found an alarm pad.

The light was green.

She let out a long breath and stepped into the apartment.

It was small, but quite spectacular. Very bright with windows on both sides of the main space. The living room featured modern furnishings; a white couch with linen chairs. A contemporary painting hung over the fireplace. The floor was polished tile that had flecks of crystal on top of a muted charcoal color. The effect was subtle but the natural light from the windows was caught and reflected in the crystal, creating a fascinating pattern that seemed to change from every angle.

To the left was a European-style kitchen with white cabinets and marble tile. To the right, a hallway that led, no doubt, to a bedroom or two and a bathroom. She opened several of the kitchen drawers and found a key card for the elevator, probably a spare, as well as a spare key to the door. Neagley slipped both of them into her pocket.

Nothing appeared to be out of place in the obvious sense.

Neagley ignored the kitchen and living room and went to the hallway. She peeked inside the small bathroom; again, a European-style sink and toilet, all ensconced in white marble tile and stainless steel fixtures. A sleek black scale sat between the toilet and the walk-in shower.

Dixon clearly preferred a home without clutter, and favored modern, contemporary design. Somehow, it made sense. A mathematical mind would find comfort in precision, Neagley reasoned.

She made her way to the first door and pushed it open.

It was a bedroom.

A queen-sized bed took up most of the space. One window occupied the main portion of the opposite wall, although a blind had been pulled down. Neagley noted the small remote control next to the bed and knew the shade was operated by the push of a button.

Very nice, she thought.

Back in the hallway, she went to the second bedroom. It featured a metal desk, made of what appeared to be airplane sheet metal, joined together by rivets. A large desktop computer faced a white leather straight-backed chair.

A contemporary couch made up of circular leather pads of different colors took up the rest of the space in the office.

Neagley sat down in the desk chair.

She immediately knew there would be little to discover elsewhere in the apartment. She would certainly check, of course, but her intuition told her anything of interest would be here, probably on the computer.

Neagley reached out and tapped a key.

The computer screen came to life.

ENTER PASSWORD.

Neagley sighed.

Chapter 8

If Dixon had a password on her computer, it would involve numbers.

Neagley was absolutely sure of that.

The problem was, numbers weren't her thing. That was strictly a Dixon/Reacher dynamic. And just like Dixon, Reacher was nowhere to be found. Probably out on the road somewhere, walking away from one town, heading for another. No phone. No email.

No, she couldn't use Reacher to help her.

One other name came to mind.

Dave O'Donnell.

He'd been a key member of the Special Investigators. A tall man, thin but sleek with muscle – they used to say he was built like a greyhound – O'Donnell had been the most fastidious of the group. Which was saying something. O'Donnell had been the best with paperwork, often volunteering to write, record and organize the team's various reports and case files. The man was also tough as nails and preferred to carry a set of brass knuckles in one pocket and a switchblade in the other.

While not a wizard with numbers like Dixon and Reacher, O'Donnell was probably her best bet for help with the password.

She scrolled through the contacts on her phone and called him.

"Neagley," he said. "What's up."

"I need help getting into Dixon's computer."

"Where's Dixon?"

"That's what I'm trying to find out."

Silence on the other end.

"It will be a series of numbers," he finally said.

"Yes."

"Did you try Reacher?"

"He's missing in action."

"I'm your second choice."

"You're my best *available* choice."

Neagley could hear O'Donnell drumming his fingers on the surface of something. Probably his desk. She smiled. O'Donnell was usually at his desk even though he preferred fieldwork. He was a man with high energy and a very active mind.

"I assume you tried all the obvious? Birthdate, military ID, phone number…"

"Yes," Neagley answered.

"How many digits?"

"Five."

More drumming.

"Both Karla and Dixon have five letters," he said. "Did you try their numerical equivalents? You know, A equals 1, B equals 2, etc."

"No."

"Okay," O'Donnell said.

Neagley heard the sound of pen scratching on paper.

"Let's start with Karla," he said. "11, 1, 18, 10, 1."

Neagley wrote down the numbers. Technically that's eight digits."

"Try the first digit of each number. That's 1, 1, 1, 1, 1, 1."

Neagley typed them in.

Incorrect password.

"What if we add them up? 11, 1, 18, 10, 1."

"That comes to 41."

O'Donnell sighed.

"Okay, let's try Dixon," he said. "4, 9, 24, 15, 14."

"I'm going to try the first digit of each."

She typed in 4, 9, 2, 1, 1.

The screen unlocked and Neagley studied the desktop.

"It worked," she said. "Unfortunately."

"Why unfortunately?"

"Because the computer's been wiped clean."

She stared at the screen. There was nothing. Not even a visible system folder on the desktop.

"Damn it," she said.

Chapter 9

"You should call Chavez," O'Donnell said.

Neagley had been unable to call anything up on Dixon's computer, despite trying everything she and O'Donnell knew in terms of computer code.

Edgar Chavez had been one of the original members of the Special Investigators and was now a well-known cyber security expert. His firm in Venice, Florida, was highly successful. Neagley had even seen Chavez quoted in national news outlets as a cyber crime expert.

She dialed his cell.

"Chavez."

"It's Neagley. I need you to help me with Karla Dixon's computer."

It was how they always operated: all business, straight to the point. Chavez didn't even waste time asking why Neagley was trying to hack her way into Dixon's computer. The answer was obvious, any explanation was not needed and would only cause a delay.

"Hold on," he said.

Neagley waited and thought she heard a clicking on the line.

"Just wanted to put on my headset so my hands are free," he said. "Okay. Shoot."

She briefly outlined the situation. Chavez asked for the name brand of the computer, which she provided.

"Okay," he said, "I'm going to give you some code to type in. Ready?"

"Ready."

He relayed a series of commands and she dutifully typed them in. Then hit the "Enter" key.

Neagley watched as a short line of code appeared and then a new cursor popped onto the screen. She read the sequence of words and numbers to Chavez.

"Shit, okay," he said. "Try this."

They repeated the process again, with a different code but it ended with the same result.

"It's toast, Neagley," Chavez said. "Someone stripped everything from it. Maybe if I had it physically in my shop here, I could try a few things. But it sounds like someone wanted to make sure it was unusable, without actually smashing it into a million pieces. They achieved the same thing, however, without the actual physical destruction."

Neagley pushed away the keyboard.

"A very thorough job," she said.

"Professional, too," Chavez pointed out. "That wasn't some junkie who deleted all the files. This was someone who knew what they were doing."

"Par for the course."

There was a pause and then Chavez said, "If you need me, I'm there. Just say the word. I think I could have some luck with that computer if I got my hands on it."

Neagley considered it, as she had with O'Donnell.

"Not yet," she said. "But I'll keep you posted."

They hung up and Neagley got to her feet, left the office and walked back out into the main room of Dixon's apartment.

She was missing something, she was sure of it.

Neagley studied the fireplace and wondered if Dixon ever used it. There was no firewood to be seen and it didn't appear to be gas operated. It was probably mostly an architectural feature, rather than a functional fireplace.

There was a painting above the mantle. It was contemporary and probably expensive. Off to her right was the hallway that led to the bedroom. There were three paintings there as well. Neagley knew enough to know that three was a prime number. Would Dixon have liked that?

She walked over and studied the three paintings.

They weren't like the one over the fireplace. These were watercolors of plants. The first two weren't signed but the third was. R. Moury.

That seemed strange to Neagley. Didn't artists sign all of their work? Why just the one? Was it a triptych? She was no art critic, but if that was the case wouldn't the three panels be connected?

Neagley stepped closer to the last painting.

R. Moury.

She'd never heard of the name. Probably some obscure artist—

Suddenly, Neagley cocked her head to one side. A word had popped into her consciousness.

Armory.

A place where weapons were stored. Every Army base had one.

Neagley carefully reached up and pulled the framed artwork toward her and peeked behind it. Nothing. Just a wall.

She went down the line and checked the other two watercolors.

Nothing behind them either.

Neagley stepped back.

The hallway wall had three paintings in a row, and then a wood trim wainscoting and below that, three squares made with wood trim painted white. Probably to provide some kind of visual aesthetic that matched the artwork above.

Neagley kneeled down and knocked gently on the first panel. It was solid.

Same with the second.

When she knocked on the third, a hollow sound echoed in the hallway. Using her fingers, she carefully felt around the wood trim that made up the square and suddenly, the panel swung open.

A small safe with a combination stared back at her.

Great, she thought.

Another puzzle.

Neagley reached out, grasped the stainless steel handle below the combination dial and pulled.

She let out a gentle breath and prayed for a small miracle.

The door swung open.

Chapter 10

The ceiling was white. As were the walls, the floor and the bedsheets.

Dixon's eyes took in the monotony of the room as her brain struggled to reconcile what she was seeing.

Not a hospital. There would be an IV or medical equipment with knobs and digital readouts, hand sanitizer and a sink, maybe even a call button for a nurse.

No, she wasn't in a hospital.

Certainly not a hotel. Not even the most ridiculously over-the-top modern hotels would dare decorate a room to resemble a cell in a sanatorium.

Perhaps that's where she was. A mental hospital.

She looked down at her body.

Jeans, black flats, a silk blouse with a distressed brown leather jacket.

If she'd been taken to some kind of institution, they probably would have put her into some kind of gown or something, not left her in her street clothes.

She patted her hip and knew that her gun was gone and she didn't see her purse anywhere.

The pain in her head at her temples told her she'd most likely been drugged. It felt vaguely like a bad hangover but Dixon knew she hadn't had anything to drink.

In her mind, she tried to go back over her last actions but it was like trying to swim in quicksand. The last thing she remembered was going home from work, unlocking her apartment, stepping inside and then…that was it.

Maybe there was a shred of memory, a fuzzy image of being in a car, on her back, staring at the roof. The sensation of being driven for some time.

But she couldn't be sure.

Her thoughts were interrupted when the wall opened and Dixon realized she hadn't even seen the white door, perfectly recessed into its invisible frame.

The visual only seemed to make the moment even more surreal for her.

A man stepped through.

Mid-fifties. Salt-and-pepper hair in a buzz cut.

A strong jaw, expensive watch and finely tailored suit.

He looked like a retired general who'd hit the big time in the private sector.

"Karla, you're awake."

Dixon watched him and then swung her feet from the bed and stood up. She felt wobbly.

From the door behind the man, two more men entered the room. They were dressed in black tactical gear and Dixon immediately noticed the pistols on their hips as well as what appeared to be canisters of pepper spray.

Even though they knew she was less than full strength they weren't taking any chances.

"Who are you? Where am I?" she asked the man. Her voice was rough and her throat scratchy. She coughed.

"You're in a safe room right now for your protection. There are people who are out to harm you and we're here to keep you safe."

Through the fog in her synapses Dixon was still able to detect the lie.

"Bullshit," she said.

A fourth person, a woman, entered the room with a tray of food and a rolling table. She was dressed in something resembling a uniform. White shirt and pants, black shoes. But she, too, had a belt with pepper spray and possibly a weapon tucked in at the small of her back.

"Eat and rest," the man said. "We'll talk again soon."

They all filed out and Dixon tried to see out the door into the hallway but it closed before she could get a glimpse.

She smelled the food and glanced at it. She was hungry but had no intention of ingesting anything they gave her.

Dixon sat back down and settled in to wait. She thought of the message she'd gotten out to Neagley and hoped her former colleague was investigating.

Dixon considered the numerical odds and began her calculations.

Chapter 11

The man who sat in a nondescript office outside of Washington, DC, and who referred to his work as "data entry" had done his job.

The information he'd collected had been sent to a second man who now sat outside Karla Dixon's apartment in New York. He was at a coffee shop, seated at an outdoor table and nursed a cappuccino while he kept an eye on the apartment building's front door.

He'd had time to go over the information sent by the member of the team who'd been tasked with electronic surveillance. There had been a series of text messages from Frances Neagley's phone to Dixon's, as well as her travel record and subsequent phone calls upon landing in New York.

Despite the bevy of information, there was no

big picture in the man's mind. He was not paid to interpret the data and form theories.

That kind of thing was well above his pay grade, as the saying went.

What he knew, instinctively, was that this was a large operation and one hand most certainly did not know what the other was doing. That was essential. Compartmentalization.

He simply knew what his job was; to alert his superior when Frances Neagley was seen leaving the building.

It was an action that took place about a half hour after he'd finished his cappuccino and refused another. The wait staff had been casting looks in his direction, hoping he'd move on and free up some premium outdoor seating space for the line of customers eager for their next installment of caffeine.

The man saw Neagley leave and he snapped a photo with his phone and sent the information to his superior.

Immediately, a text reply appeared on his phone.

Follow her.

Chapter 12

Neagley looked at the single sheet of paper inside the safe.

She was reminded of the scene from one of the Indiana Jones movies, when the main character sees a pit filled with snakes, which he loathed and feared, and said, "Snakes. Why did it have to be snakes?"

Neagley studied the sheet of papers and all she saw were numbers. Rows and rows of numbers. And she thought to herself, *Numbers. Why does it have to be numbers?*

But what took her breath away was the number at the very bottom of the columns and off to the side. It was handwritten, unlike all of the others, which appeared to have been typed into a spreadsheet.

It was written in red ink and Neagley thought

she recognized Dixon's unique handwriting. It was all block capital letters, but Dixon's always looked slightly feminized with the occasional curve.

The number was not small.

$500,000,000.00

Five hundred million dollars.

Neagley let out a long, low whistle. This wasn't beer money Dixon had been dealing with. And why had she put a spreadsheet into a hidden safe? Was it Dixon who'd put it there? Or had the people who'd wiped her computer clean also discovered the safe, and planted the sheet of paper there? Maybe it was a false lead. Misdirection.

For some reason, Neagley didn't think so.

She turned the paper over in her hands but the other side was blank.

Neagley turned the sheet back over and studied the numbers. In addition to the whopper in the lower right, there were four distinct rows of numbers, and one number at the top.

26 7201.

Another puzzle. Neagley looked at the number at the top out of the corner of her eyes. It was the space between the 26 and the 7201 that made her wonder. She felt like it was the most important thing about it.

The silence of the apartment hung over Neagley. She suddenly became aware of the space, of the situation and her role within it.

She used her phone and took a photograph of the sheet and its contents, then folded the paper and tucked it into a pocket.

Neagley carefully shut the safe, closed the hidden door and left Dixon's apartment.

She had already made a decision, but wasn't quite ready to act on it.

They'd only done it once before, and she was hesitant to do it again.

But if Dixon was missing and it had something to do with five hundred million dollars, she might not have a choice.

It was time to once again reunite the Special Investigators.

Chapter 13

The man was glad he chose not to use the coffee shop's restroom. Because just as he was about to surrender to the needs of his bladder, Frances Neagley emerged from Karla Dixon's apartment building.

He waited until she had turned to walk down the street away from him before he got to his feet and hurried after.

The man stuck a phone to his ear and speed dialed his superior.

"She's on the move, I assume back to where she parked her car."

"Stand by, Waters is two blocks away," the voice on the other end of the line told him. "He'll pick you up. The two of you follow her but absolutely do not risk exposure."

With Neagley still in sight, the man rolled

his eyes. "Of course," he said, trying and succeeding to keep the irritation out of his voice. What, did they think he was an amateur? That he couldn't follow some random woman without being seen?

Ridiculous.

He disconnected the call and stayed on the opposite side of the street. His target seemed to be walking briskly but not in a panic.

Moments later, a black Cadillac sedan stopped just past him and he climbed into the front passenger seat.

Waters was a slim black man with a Bluetooth earpiece in place. They nodded at each other and continued on.

"She parked her car there," the man from the coffee shop, whose name was Brandt, said.

"Not ideal, but we'll manage," Waters said. He retrieved a handicapped parking sticker from the glove compartment and pulled into a spot a block from the office building Frances Neagley had entered, with the parking garage's exit in view.

They didn't have to wait long.

Brandt watched as his target pulled out of the parking garage and headed south. Waters followed and neither man spoke until the woman finally veered into the valet entrance to an upscale Soho hotel.

Brandt spoke into his phone. "She pulled into a hotel. Valet."

His superior responded immediately. "Leave Waters, go inside and make sure she checks into a room. Send me the information when you have it."

Brandt disconnected the call, shrugged off his sport coat to alter his appearance and left the vehicle. Neither he nor Waters spoke.

Inside the hotel, he saw the woman at the front desk with only a leather bag over her shoulder. He walked into the bar area that offered a sight line toward the elevators. Brandt ordered a mineral water with a lime.

He didn't even have a chance to take a drink before his target left the front desk and headed for the elevator. He waited until she was inside and made another call.

"She's checked in."

Brandt listened as the voice on the other end of the line gave him his new orders.

Chapter 14

The news report was labeled with big white letters against a red bar: BREAKING NEWS.

Three men dead in a parking lot outside a blue-collar bar in Virginia.

Their friend, a woman, found dead in a cheap motel room a mile away. She'd been the victim of a brutal assault.

The police had a suspect and physical description, but no photograph.

The man responsible for those murders watched the story with neither amusement nor fear. He sat with his shirt off, the tattoo ACE reflected in the mirror across the room.

He thought about that night, how he'd made eye contact with the woman, what was her name? Connie. He smiled. Joe and his buddies had tried to jump him and he'd butchered them like cattle at a slaughterhouse.

Then he'd taken Connie to a hotel, not the one he was currently staying at, and brutalized her, too. He'd worked on her all night, without tiring, until the loss of blood had finally caused her organs to shut down.

He stood and stretched. He wasn't used to inactivity. Ace needed to move, to work, to attack something, anything.

The morning light filtered in through the window by the door. The curtains were white, cheap and flimsy so he hadn't bothered closing them. He got to his feet and studied his reflection.

Perfect.

It was the only word that came to mind. Chiseled muscle. Not a mark on his body, other than the tattoo.

The girl he'd killed in the room, she'd scratched him a number of times but those marks were healed and long gone. His crotch stirred at her memory; his senses had never been more alive and he'd savored every adrenaline-inducing moment.

Ace didn't know all the ins and outs of what was going on, but he knew he wanted more. More violence. More sex. More thrills.

But he had to set that aside. The incident at

the bar had come about accidentally and he'd simply gone with it.

He'd been on his way to do a job.

And that work still remained unfinished.

His life depended on finding the man who held the key to his survival.

And for Ace, time was running out.

Chapter 15

Neagley knew she was being followed.

The problem was, she didn't exactly spot her tail. There'd been a man on the street near Dixon's office building, and then a man who looked very similar had appeared in the hotel at the bar, but she hadn't been completely certain. Perhaps it was the same man or maybe he'd altered his look.

In any event, she'd made note of his face and there wouldn't be any confusion if she saw him again.

Neagley checked into her room – a junior suite with a sitting area that consisted of a couch, two chairs, and a bookcase where a television sat. A desk was off to one side and she took her laptop from her bag, plugged the computer into a charging strip and went into the bedroom.

She stripped off her clothes, showered, changed into loose-fitting workout pants and a black T-shirt and went back to the computer.

On the desk, she placed the sheet of paper from Dixon's safe.

26 7201.

The numbers meant nothing to her.

Did 26 mean the 26th? Of what month?

If it was a date, did it mean 01/26/72? January 26, 1972?

That made no sense.

It couldn't possibly be a combination to a safe, as it was *in* a safe.

Neagley looked at her computer, and then down at her phone. Reacher used to always tell her not to overthink things. That sometimes the obvious thing was the true thing.

Try as she might, she couldn't ignore the fact that Dixon was missing, her apartment had clearly been searched and sanitized, she was involved with something consisting of very high stakes – to the tune of half a billion dollars.

On top of that, she'd been sent a 1030 by a woman who was as close to a sister as she'd ever had.

Neagley knew she could work on the computer, use her resources, try to come up with some possible leads or avenues of investigation.

But she knew she was overthinking it.

Dixon was missing and needed her help.

And right now, Neagley was at a crossroads.

She knew she needed help, too.

Dave O'Donnell. Edgar Chavez. Allan Cooper.

Don't overthink it.

Including her, but not including Reacher, they were the last of the Special Investigators.

Neagley didn't know if she needed them all, or even if any of them were able to help.

Reacher's voice was in her head: *don't overthink it. You need them. Make the call.*

Thirty minutes later, she'd spoken to all three of them and within twenty-four hours, they would all be in New York.

To help her find Karla Dixon.

Chapter 16

Dixon had run the numbers and they weren't very good.

Her odds of getting out of this thing intact diminished every minute she sat here doing squat.

On your feet soldier, she told herself.

Dixon stood and began to pace the empty room. They'd left the food and water tray but she hadn't touched it. The hunger pangs were definitely intensifying but she could go longer without food. Soon, though, she would have to drink. Her throat was parched.

The important thing was to think and to investigate. That's what she'd been, after all. One of the Special Investigators. Their motto had always been *you do not mess with the Special Investigators*. She didn't know who'd come up with it, but everyone had embraced it. And with Reacher as the leader of the group, well, he carried a certain physical presence with him at all times. Extremely intimidating.

Now, she felt the memory of that period of her life and instantly felt stronger.

It had all started so innocently; she'd found an anomaly in a subsidiary, that was all. She'd pulled a string, and then another one had come undone, and soon, she was in the middle of something totally unexpected and under surveillance.

There'd been no time, other than to dash off a postcard to Neagley.

Now, Dixon felt a sense of guilt. She was captive, and there might be people putting themselves at great risk to help. And they had no idea what they were up against. She had to get out. Had to escape.

Dixon paced the room, studying its construction. Standard drywall. Tight seams. Minimal shoe molding. Tile floor probably over cement. The ceiling was plaster, with recessed lighting. The door fit neatly into the wall, its frame nearly invisible. No way to get a finger in there and pry, not that it would have done any good anyway.

No windows.

Dixon went back and looked at the tray of food and water. The tray was made of dull aluminum. The plate was plastic as was the cup.

"It tastes better than it looks," a voice said behind her.

She turned and the man with the buzz cut was back. Dixon was impressed the door had opened without a single sound.

"That's not saying much," she responded.

Dixon turned to face him.

Her body had tensed and the door was still open behind him.

He put a hand up.

"Don't do what you're clearly thinking," he said. "You have no need to attack me or bull rush me. There are three more people just outside the room and the doors at each end of the hallway are locked. Even if you got by me, which you wouldn't, you'd have nowhere to go."

"Maybe I just want to hurt someone," she said.

"Understandable. But there's another reason you don't have to try to escape this room."

She waited.

"We'll happily let you out." He stepped aside and gestured toward the door.

"Let's go. Someone wants to talk to you."

Chapter 17

There were plenty of things he could change about himself, but some he couldn't.

For instance, his overall physicality.

Ace was a big man. Six feet four inches, broad shoulders, muscular arms and a powerful lower body. Without the use of prosthetics to either make himself even taller, or more likely, to make him look heavier, even overweight, there wasn't much he could do. He didn't have any of that kind of equipment with him.

What he did have was a razor, and he'd managed to nab a pair of scissors from the front desk at the hotel.

In his room, he chopped off most of his hair and shaved the sides of his head. He left some stubble on his face and fashioned it into a goatee.

His clothes were a problem, too. In the

description the local news station had broadcast, they'd pretty much gotten his clothes right. That, combined with his physical appearance, would make him easily identifiable.

Luckily, he'd passed a Walmart not far from where he'd ended up, and he could use what little cash he had to buy a new T-shirt and baseball cap. Maybe even a pair of sunglasses. He doubted they would have people watching retail stores.

More likely, they'd be watching military supply stores, bus lines, train stations and the airport.

A Walmart in semi-rural Virginia? No way.

Besides, they had a pretty good idea of where he was going and would have people there waiting. The rest was window dressing for the local authorities, to throw them off the trail of what was really happening.

In the meantime, he was fairly safe to move around.

The local police were looking for him, but he wasn't worried about that. If they had the misfortune to actually stumble their way upon him, they were no match for his size and skill.

His former "team" though? They would be a handful, that was certain.

He checked his watch.

This was the ideal time. Late morning. Plenty of people around.

He packed up his few belongings, went out to his car and started it up.

The Walmart wasn't busy at all and he bought himself a T-shirt that had a picture of a deer on the front with the words "Buck Fever" across the top. For his hat, he chose a baseball cap that said *Miller Time*. For sunglasses, he found a thick black pair that reminded him of Arnold Schwarzenegger in the Terminator.

Ace made his purchase, went into the store's bathroom, took off his shirt and threw it into the trash. He put on his new Buck Fever T-shirt, baseball cap and cheap sunglasses and walked back out to the car.

He knew where he was going and planned to do some basic reconnaissance. They would be watching for him, so he would have to be creative.

Ace smiled.

When it came to killing a person, any person, there were always challenges.

But so far, he had always found a way.

Chapter 18

Coffee was the first order of business.

Neagley had commandeered each of the men a room, but had also grabbed one of the hotel's small conference rooms. She'd arranged to have several pots of coffee placed in the room, along with some fruit and breakfast pastries.

All the while, she kept an eye out for the man who she thought might have been watching her, but she saw no sign of him.

If she knew her team, they wouldn't want to waste too much time. Rather, they would want to begin the hunt for Dixon immediately.

Dave O'Donnell was the first to arrive. He came into the conference room looking like a native New Yorker. He wore a perfectly tailored suit, a Rolex Submariner and Neagley knew that in one of his pockets he had a switchblade knife.

In the other would be a set of brass knuckles made with a ceramic material.

O'Donnell was built like a greyhound; tall, lean and whipcord strong. He had sandy-colored hair with a modern cut, and looked like he might be a Wall Street executive or a partner in a law firm.

Neagley knew despite his polished looks, Dave was one of the toughest of them all. Not a person you want to meet in a dark alley at night looking for trouble.

"Neagley," he said as he entered the room.

They made no move to hug or shake hands. Neagley wasn't fond of touching other people and everyone in the squad knew this and respected her feelings. She'd never told anyone why she was that way, and never planned to. It was her business and hers alone.

"You track down Reacher?" he asked.

"No luck."

"Who else?"

"Coop and Chavez." Coop was Allan Cooper's nickname. "Their arrival times were close so they're sharing a cab and should both be here any minute."

O'Donnell nodded and made a beeline for the coffee. He poured himself a cup and added no sugar or cream. He glanced at the pastries but must not have seen anything he liked because he turned back to Neagley.

"How have you been?"

"Fine. You?"

"Business is too good," O'Donnell said. He ran his own private investigation practice in the DC area. "Have to decide if I want to expand or not. But then I'd be management. I hate sitting behind a desk."

O'Donnell had always been the best report writer on the team and when precise paperwork had been needed, they'd always counted on him.

Just then, the door opened and Allan Cooper's bulk filled the frame.

Coop was the only person who had come close to matching Reacher in terms of physical size and strength. Cooper was six-and-a-half feet tall and three hundred pounds. Although massive, he didn't carry as much body fat as one would expect. He was bald and his white teeth gleamed as his face broke into a smile.

"Damn Neagley, you don't ever change," he said. His voice was a rich baritone and he crossed the room, shook hands with O'Donnell as Chavez entered the conference room and closed the door.

"Hey Neagley," Chavez said. He was probably the most intelligent of the group, and somewhat soft spoken by nature. But Neagley knew Chavez had grown up on the mean streets of Dallas and was lightning quick with a knife. A crack shot, too, but then again they all were. Even though no one could beat Reacher on the range.

He, too, crossed the room and shook hands with O'Donnell. More coffee was poured and soon, the four of them sat down at the round conference room table. Coop was shoveling pastries into his mouth, spilling crumbs onto the table. Chavez had two phones on the table in front of him.

O'Donnell leaned back in his chair and waited for Neagley to begin.

"It started with a 1030 from Dixon," she said.

Chapter 19

Neagley took them through everything she'd done. O'Donnell already knew about Dixon's computer as he'd been the one who'd helped solve the puzzle that eventually led to its unlocking. And Chavez had helped determine the computer had been wiped. All of it was new to Cooper.

"And you said half a *billion*, right? Not half a million," the big man said.

"A five and eight zeros," Neagley said. "Half a billion."

"What do we know about Dixon's job? Did she deal with this kind of money on a regular basis?" Chavez asked.

"Possibly," Neagley answered. "She worked for a firm called FT Investigations. According to their website they specialize in financial matters like forensic accounting. But in terms of the size of their budgets and the amount of money they deal with, I don't know. That's something we need to find out."

O'Donnell got to his feet and paced. He was like that; full of energy all the time. "If she sent you a coded message, she knew she was already under surveillance. She knew someone was watching her, watching what she said and did."

Neagley nodded, indicating he should continue.

"Considering who Dixon is and her capabilities, that automatically means this isn't a single person involved. Dixon could easily shake a single watcher. But for her to go through that level of complexity to contact you means there was a high degree of sophistication involved. Electronic as well as human."

"Where there's half a billion dollars involved, there's going to be lots of eyes on it," Chavez said.

Cooper pushed away the plate of pastries and drained his coffee.

"What I don't get," he said, "is why Dixon?"

"What do you mean?" Chavez asked.

"Look, whatever the hell is going on with this money, it's bigger than Karla Dixon. Hell, I'm doing protective services in LA for celebrities who are worth maybe twenty or thirty million dollars. All kinds of people have their fingers in the pie. A half billion? There's gotta be armies of folks running around. So what I'm saying is Dixon can't be the only person at the center of this thing. If it's something to do with her company, then there have to be others there we can talk to."

"Conversely," O'Donnell said. "If this has nothing to do with her day job, then we have to know that, too. Because that means she's got some other kind of business on the side that's enormous. Like, ridiculously huge."

Chavez held up the sheet of paper Neagley had found in Dixon's safe. The neat rows of numbers with the single number at the top.

"I want to tackle this," he said. "And Dixon's computer."

"I thought you said it was wiped clean," O'Donnell pointed out.

"It was," Neagley said.

"I brought some stuff that might help," Chavez said. "It's hard to delete every last thing from a computer without completely destroying it. The fact that it's still there in Dixon's apartment is a good sign. I'm hoping it will tell me something."

The room was quiet for a moment.

Neagley knew what they were thinking. Reacher was usually in charge; he was the one who would ultimately determine a course of action. He wasn't around. Someone needed to fill the void.

As if it were a choreographed move, all three men turned to Neagley.

"O'Donnell and Cooper, I want you to handle Dixon's workplace," she said. "Do what you have to do to find out if this involves FT Investigations. One way or another, we need to know."

"We can do that," O'Donnell said.

"I'm going to work with Chavez," Neagley said. "He's going to need me to get back into Dixon's apartment anyway."

"I didn't bring anything with me," Cooper said. "Regulations, you know."

"That's not a problem," Neagley answered. She knew he was talking about guns. "My company has a branch here and I was able to request all the equipment we need. It's in my room."

Cooper smiled. "You do not mess with the Special Investigators."

Chavez headed for the door. "And if you do, you are dead men walking."

Chapter 20

He was reminded of the childhood game *monkey in the middle*.

Not that he'd ever played it; he didn't even know what the game consisted of. The phrase, at the moment, seemed appropriate.

Mostly because of his stature.

Or, more accurately, the lack of it.

He was a small man. Well under six feet and he probably weighed one hundred forty pounds soaking wet. His shoulders were narrow and bowed inward. His hair was thinning and what remained fell to one side, and he had a nervous habit of pushing it back toward the middle.

So, in this scenario, he was the monkey.

But what was he in the middle of?

He glanced and estimated he was surrounded

by nearly two thousand pounds – a full ton – of flesh, muscle and bone.

Six big men, all of them giants and most likely three hundred pounds each were posted at various positions around his house. Three outside. Three inside. All of them armed with gleaming machine guns, pistols and knives.

In the house, one was near the front door, one stationed at the back, and the other seemed to be a free agent, always on the move. He went upstairs, downstairs, into the kitchen, back to the living room, into the bathrooms, and then he would start the whole circuit again.

Now, the little man, known to his colleagues as Dr. Pribbenow, retreated to his study. It was the one place the bodyguards were not allowed.

Pribbenow locked the door behind him and went to his computer.

He hated what his life had become.

All because what so many people had claimed about him was true: he was a genius. As in, off-the-charts brilliant. His few detractors, who said his ideas were too outlandish and unrealistic, had quietly disappeared.

It didn't matter, though.

It was too late now.

He was going to die.

They were *all* going to die.

Chapter 21

"Man, she's still like that," Coop said.

O'Donnell knew instantly what he was talking about. "Yeah, you don't mess with us, but you really don't mess with Frances Neagley."

They were walking into the building that housed Dixon's employer: FT Investigations.

"You ever ask what it was all about? The no touching?"

"Nope. Don't intend to, either."

After a pause, Cooper said, "Yeah, me neither."

O'Donnell found the building directory.

"So what's new in LA?" O'Donnell asked as they walked toward the elevators. "You still guarding Beyoncé or Shakira or Rihanna?"

"What, you only know one-name female entertainers, O'Donnell?"

"Nah, I just figured that's the type of client you would aim for."

"Cute," Coop said. "But no. I mostly provide security for Silicon Valley guys. They make, like, ten times as much coin as the Hollywood stars. How 'bout you?"

"Not as much glamour, but business is good," O'Donnell said. "Ever hear from Reacher?"

"You kiddin' me? The man turned into a ghost."

"Yeah, I always figure one day he's going to waltz into my office looking like a homeless bum and ask if I want to grab a cup of coffee and some pie."

"That's about his style these days, from what I hear."

O'Donnell punched the appropriate floor's number in the elevator. When the doors closed, Cooper said, "So how do you want to play this?"

They were both armed. After the meeting in the conference room they had all retreated to Neagley's room where she'd broken out a military case containing mostly Glocks. They'd each taken one.

"Let's refer to ourselves as Cagney and Lacey," O'Donnell said.

"How 'bout Simon and Simon?"

The doors opened and O'Donnell stepped out

first. He took in the expansive lobby, marble floors and headed straight for the front desk.

He pulled out his leather ID holder which held his private investigator license and showed it to the receptionist.

"My partner and I are here to investigate a case involving Karla Dixon. May we please speak to her supervisor?"

"Mm, hold on one minute, please."

The young man turned his back on O'Donnell and spoke into his headset. He seemed intimidated by them, especially by Cooper. When he turned back, O'Donnell thought the young man's thin moustache was quivering just a bit. "If you want to take a seat, Mary Parra will be out to see you."

"Is she Dixon's supervisor?"

"Um, yes, but a different department."

"Which department?"

"Human Resources," a voice said.

A door behind the reception area and off to O'Donnell's right had opened. A stocky brunette woman was looking at him.

She motioned for O'Donnell and Cooper to follow, which they did.

Parra led them to a conference room. Inside sat a man with an expensive silk suit, but his tie was loosened and he had a fatigued expression on his face.

"Please sit down, gentlemen," Parra said.

They introduced themselves and O'Donnell was pleased they didn't press him on what kind of investigators they were. He had been very careful not to actually say they were with law enforcement. Then again, if FT Investigations had their act together, they might have been able to put two and two together and realize they were former colleagues of Dixon's. Either way, Parra and the guy in the suit didn't seem to be very curious, which set off a red flag in O'Donnell's mind.

She asked, "Can I get you a bottled water?"

"No thanks," O'Donnell said.

"This is Ariel Yost," Parra said, gesturing to the man. "He oversaw Karla Dixon's work."

"Why are you using the past tense?" Cooper asked. "She doesn't work here anymore?"

"Ms. Dixon has taken a leave of absence."

"What kind of work did she do for you?"

Yost looked at Parra who nodded, giving him permission to speak, O'Donnell assumed.

"Forensic accounting, in the broader sense," Yost said. "Karla was the best I've ever seen. It's a shame if she doesn't return."

"What specifically was she working on?" Cooper probed.

"We are not at liberty to discuss client information. We have a very strict confidentiality agreement with all of our partners," Parra said.

"What kind of numbers are we talking about?" O'Donnell asked.

"I'm not sure what you mean," Yost said.

"I mean, your clients' financials, are we talking millions? Tens of millions? Hundreds of millions?"

"We work with many multinational organizations," Parra said. "Yes to all of those."

"What specifically was Dixon's job?"

Again, Parra deferred to Yost.

"Karla was in charge of detecting financial anomalies. A little bit like quality control. While she wasn't necessarily responsible for say, preparing a client's tax return or audit, she was involved in identifying possible problem areas. A troubleshooter of sorts."

"And what would happen if she found an anomaly?"

"We bring it to our client's attention, of course."

"You wouldn't investigate on your own?"

"Oh God no," Yost said. "We're accountants, nothing more. We have no criminal division or investigative arm. All we can do is supply the information to our clients and it's up to them to decide what to do with it."

"Did Dixon find any anomalies recently?"

"We can't say one way or the other," Parra answered.

"Did she say why she needed a leave of absence?" Cooper asked.

"No. It was a rather formal request that caught us off guard, to be honest." Parra looked directly at O'Donnell. "It seemed somewhat out of character. We reached out to Karla but haven't heard back."

Yost straightened up in his chair. "Dixon is the best forensic accountant I've ever worked with. If she needs our help, anything we can do, we'll do it."

He got up and nodded to Parra.

"Let me show you out," she said.

Chapter 22

Getting back into Dixon's apartment was a much easier process.

Neagley had pocketed the spare key card for the elevator as well as the door to Dixon's apartment so she and Chavez were able to simply walk in, take the elevator up and let themselves in.

Easy.

"Nice place," Chavez said as he took in the view and the size of Dixon's home.

"Computer's in here," Neagley said, leading him to the room down the hall.

Chavez followed and looked at the desktop computer.

"I'm going to copy everything first, and then dismantle it and bring the hard drive with us," he said. "It'll probably take me a half hour or so."

"Okay."

Neagley left him in the room and she continued to look around the apartment. She went back to the secret compartment, opened it, and looked in the safe. It was empty.

She closed everything up and went into Dixon's bedroom. The closet was full of high-end clothes, mostly work, with a separate section for exercise gear. Dixon had clearly committed to staying in shape.

In the bathroom Neagley found a variety of skin care products along with the usual assortment of shampoos, soaps and conditioners.

Next to the bed was a nightstand with a drawer. She opened it up, found lube and a pack of condoms. Also, a romance novel.

Neagley shut the drawer and ventured into the kitchen and then the living room.

Nothing was out of place, and nothing seemed to be missing. She was a little surprised by Dixon's lack of personal effects. There just wasn't much. Not a lot of family photos and keepsakes. Neagley chalked it up to life in the military. It tended to prevent the accumulation of objects. Reacher, for example. He had taken decluttering to an art form. His sole possessions were an ATM card, passport, toothbrush and the clothes on his back.

Chavez appeared in the doorway. He was stuffing a piece of computer equipment into his leather backpack.

"I may have found something," he said.

He came and sat in a chair next to Neagley.

"While the hard drive was copying over, I cut and pasted the numbers from Dixon's spreadsheet into a database."

"What kind of database?"

"It's basically a collection of information known to be involved in crimes. It's mostly used for computer people like me. It's number based and what we're usually looking for are specific types of codes used by hackers."

"That makes sense. Dixon investigates financial crimes. I'm sure she came into contact with hackers all the time."

"But it's more than that. This virtual warehouse also contains numbers like offshore bank accounts, stolen credit card numbers, phone numbers, even complex algorithms used to manipulate stock exchanges."

"So you got a hit?"

"Not exactly."

"What then?"

"What I found were thousands of crimes from all over the world. Different industries, too. But they all had one number in common."

Neagley remembered the number at the top of Dixon's spreadsheet. "26 7201."

"That's right. 26 7201."

She waited. "What the hell is the number? A bank account? Hacker code? What?"

Chavez gave a puzzled smile. "It's a government code for a certain crime."

"The government?"

"Yeah, the IRS."

"For what crime?"

"Tax evasion."

Chapter 23

O'Donnell glanced at Coop. "Thoughts?" he asked.

They had just exited Dixon's office building after meeting with her boss and the company's HR person.

"No reason not to take what they're saying at face value," Coop ventured. "But…"

"But Dixon is still missing."

"Exactly."

They crossed the street and began walking in the general direction of Neagley's hotel. O'Donnell knew they could call a cab, but he wanted to walk and talk. He was tired of sitting. He needed action.

"I believe them when they say it's not their job to investigate – that if they uncover discrepancies in their clients' books, they simply alert them,"

Coop reasoned. "But that doesn't explain someone grabbing Dixon. If that was all they did, why would they want her? Seems to me that kind of thing would be a last resort, and it would be aimed at the person who was actively investigating them. If Dixon's job was to only alert a client to a discrepancy, all they would have to do is ignore it. End of story. No reason to grab her."

"Exactly. And if that's the case, *who* would want her?" O'Donnell asked. "If she uncovered some kind of accounting anomaly in one of her clients' businesses, they would be the ones who would want to talk to her. And they could, because she would have alerted them in the first place."

"We need to find out what company she was working for and ask them. Maybe they got the tip from Dixon, and took it somewhere. And wherever they went with it, or to whomever they went, maybe they grabbed her."

"That's not all we need to find out," Coop said.

"You mean the guy who's following us?"

O'Donnell had spotted him a block ago. Just on the periphery of his vision.

"Yep. Turn here."

There was an alleyway between a deli and a store selling bamboo baskets. O'Donnell stepped into the alley, pushed his hand into his pocket and slid his fingers into the brass knuckles.

Cooper stood just behind him.

Moments later, a shadow briefly paused outside the alley's entrance and then a face peered in.

O'Donnell lashed out with his hand and grabbed the man by the throat, spinning him and crashing him into the brick wall.

It was Ariel Yost. "Please don't kill me!" he shouted, his eyes wide with terror.

He'd grunted with pain as his body had slammed into the stone.

O'Donnell hoped he hadn't hurt him too bad.

"Why are you following us?" Coop asked.

Yost looked terrified. Cooper was a huge man and even more intimidating up close. O'Donnell had his fist back, the set of razor-sharp knuckles poised to crash into the captive's face.

"Look, I would get fired if they knew I said something," Yost whined.

"You're scared of that Parra woman?" Coop asked, his voice slightly taunting. O'Donnell knew he was baiting him.

"Not just her. HR! They're like the fricking Gestapo."

"Yeah, well, they're not here now, pal, so you can either cough up some information or you'll be spitting out some teeth. Your choice."

Yost let out a ragged breath. "Drugs."

"What do you mean, drugs?"

"Money and drugs – the two don't go together!" Yost said, his tone belligerent.

O'Donnell forced himself to take a breath.

"Okay, why don't you try to make some sense, Yost? Start from the beginning."

"I can't, I have to go," Yost said. "I think someone followed me from the building."

"No one followed you," Cooper said. "We saw you following us and we would've seen someone if they put a tail on you."

"Why don't you relax?" O'Donnell said. He loosened his grip on Yost and the man pushed off slightly from the wall and straightened his tie, ran his hands down his now somewhat wrinkled suit.

"Seriously, I have to get back. They're going to know I'm gone," Yost said. "Dixon made a connection to Adria and apparently someone made a threat to kneecap–"

Pfft.

The sound came from outside the alley and O'Donnell knew what it was, just as Yost's head exploded in a shower of blood and gore.

Someone firing a pistol with a silencer.

An assassin.

O'Donnell dove for cover. He went one way, Cooper went the other.

They both drew their Glocks and hurried past what was left of Yost. O'Donnell couldn't help but glance at the man – his beautiful silver suit was drenched in blood. So much for his fear of Human Resources.

O'Donnell ducked around the corner, but the street was clear. "Shit," he said.

"Where'd the shot come from?" Coop asked.

"I think right here, or in the street. We couldn't see them, but they got an angle on Yost."

They both glanced back at the dead man.

"Dave," Coop said. "We gotta go."

They hurried from the alley, hustled down several street blocks and then hailed a cab and gave the driver the name of Neagley's hotel.

O'Donnell glanced down at his shirt.

Some of Yost's blood had splattered his expensive suit. He felt bad for the dead man, not only because he was probably innocent, but because he probably had more information to tell them. Now, he would never have the chance.

Coop noticed O'Donnell's blood-stained suit, too.

"That's why I don't spend that kind of money on clothes. Not in our line of work."

At that moment, O'Donnell couldn't argue with him.

Chapter 24

Neagley and Chavez left Dixon's apartment and made their way back to Neagley's hotel. They set up shop in Chavez's room while he hooked up Dixon's hard drive to his own computer and typed away with a barely controlled fury on the keyboard.

"So Dixon found out someone was cheating on their taxes?" Neagley asked. "That's what this is all about?" Neagley asked. She stood behind Chavez and watched him work.

"It would seem that way."

Chavez's screen was blank and then suddenly, lines of code began to appear.

"Ordinarily, that wouldn't be a big deal. But we're talking about half a billion dollars," Neagley reasoned. "That's a lot of money. I wonder if it's how much they cheated, or how much their income was. If the amount they shaved off their taxes was five hundred mil, imagine how much their actual revenue was. What kind of businesses bring in that much?"

Chavez leaned back in his chair and studied his screen.

None of what she saw made sense to Neagley.

"Pharmaceuticals," he said. Chavez leaned forward and tapped his keyboard. The screen froze. He pointed at a word buried in the text in all caps.

SANZER.

"SANZER? I've never heard of them."

Chavez had an iPad next to the laptop and he swiped at its screen. A website came up. Sanzer Pharmaceuticals.

"What's weird is that Dixon's hard drive was mostly wiped clean," Chavez explained. "The only mistake they made was they searched the drive after they'd wiped it. And they searched for only one word: SANZER. It's the only thing that survived. The very thing they were trying to hide."

Neagley studied the iPad and read out loud: "Sanzer Pharmaceuticals was formed in 2012 as a leading innovator in advanced medical solutions." She clicked on some of the other website tabs but they contained little else.

"Pretty skimpy on the information," Chavez pointed out. There were some stock photographs of lab technicians, as well as copyright information. A few generic press releases on new guidelines within the industry. But no photos of executives or an actual address. No specific mentions of products, or company events, or even links to learn more about the executives. There was a contact form to fill out in order to request more information.

Neagley forwarded the website to her assistant back in Chicago with instructions to find out everything they could on Sanzer.

She picked up the spreadsheet from Dixon's safe. So the numbers at the top were an IRS code for tax evasion. Something Dixon hadn't wanted to spell out, apparently. The itemized amounts were, what, recurring payments? Cash deposits? Payoffs?

"Ah Dixon," Neagley said, exasperated, wishing her friend was there. "You're the only one who can make sense of this. And you're the one we're looking for."

"The headquarters for Sanzer are in Virginia," Chavez said. He wrote down an address. "Let's go and kick some ass. If they've done anything to her, they are dead men walking."

Neagley followed him out the door.

On the way to the elevator, she took out her cell phone and dialed Dave O'Donnell.

Before anyone answered, the elevator doors opened.

O'Donnell and Cooper stepped out.

Chapter 25

"We need to regroup," O'Donnell said.

"Is that blood?" Neagley asked.

They turned and went back to Neagley's room. She unlocked the door and they all filed in.

"You first," she said.

O'Donnell explained what he and Cooper had learned at FT Investigations and the subsequent conversation with Ariel Yost before he was murdered.

"That lines up with what we found," Chavez said. He filled them in on Sanzer Pharmaceuticals. "That's where we were headed. Their headquarters are in Virginia, just outside of DC."

"Was there any mention of a woman named Adria?" Coop asked. "Yost said Dixon had made a connection with her and then he said something really strange – that someone had made a threat to kneecap someone. I'm assuming he meant Dixon."

"Weird word – that's usually what you think of when you're talking about the Irish mob. Ever hear of the Belfast six pack?" O'Donnell asked. "Bullets in both kneecaps, both elbows and both ankles."

"Ouch," Chavez replied.

"Pack your bags, boys," Neagley said. "And get rid of that suit, O'Donnell. You really shouldn't spend so much money on clothes in our line of work."

"That's what I said," Coop added.

"Keep your weapons, we're going to drive down. No time for the airport; I'll have the car out front in ten. Let's go, time's wasting."

Chapter 26

Dixon was brought into another room. Similar to the one she'd just come from. But this one had an actual door, a window and a table and chairs.

There was also a mirror.

Behind that mirror was the older man with the buzzcut, the expensive watch and the tailored suit, Dixon was certain. The one Dixon had assumed was a retired general who'd made it big in the private sector.

She wasn't far off.

His name was Bancroft. While not a general, he'd been in command of various military units over the years. He himself had transitioned from the service two years ago and was now acting as a liaison on a project far bigger and far more important than he'd ever dealt with before.

Now, he studied Dixon from behind the two-way mirror.

"This is a goddamn mess," he said.

He turned to the others in the room. They were standing around with their hands in their pockets, or checking their phones, anything to avoid eye contact with Bancroft.

"If you idiots had her under close surveillance before the grab, how did she manage to alert the others? And how much did Yost tell them before we took him out?"

The other people in the room stayed silent.

"Useless. Totally useless," Bancroft said in a matter-of-fact tone.

"Bring Dr. P back here right now," he said. "Ace isn't taking the bait. And send the ones guarding him off to intercept Neagley and her team. We need to nip this thing in the bud."

He glared at the men who'd dared to meet his eye. "And don't screw this up," he said as he left the room. He walked out into the hall, opened the first door on the left and stepped inside.

Karla Dixon looked up at him.

"Dixon, we need to talk," he said.

A small smile appeared on her face.

"You seem tense," she said. "Not like before. Why is that?"

Bancroft wanted to slap her, but he restrained himself. She was going to die eventually, and he had no problem with inflicting violence on women, but he'd be damned if he'd show a loss of control to her and his team.

"How did you manage to get word to Neagley?" he asked.

She cocked her head to one side. "Who?"

Bancroft chuckled.

"Oh, you're going to play it like that?" he asked. "Please don't insult my intelligence."

"Then don't insult mine."

He took a deep breath. "Here's how it's going to go. You're going to tell me exactly what information you managed to convey to Frances Neagley. If we determine it's harmless, she'll live. If we decide otherwise, she'll die. In the most horrific way possible."

Now it was Dixon's turn to laugh. "Have you ever heard of Jack Reacher?"

Bancroft's silence answered her question.

"6'5" tall, built like a gorilla. He hits first, and he hits hard. I've seen him demolish an entire street gang all by himself."

"I'm not interested in Jack Reacher. I'm interested in Frances Neagley."

"Well, do you know the only person in the world Jack Reacher feared?"

Again, Bancroft was silent.

"Yeah, that's right. Neagley. So you can stand here and make threats about what you're going to do to her, but I gotta tell you, it's all complete bullshit. Neagley will chew you up and spit you out, then grind what's left of you into the dirt with her boot heel. That goes for you and all of your little buddies back there hiding behind the glass playing grab ass with each other."

Dixon studied the mirror across from her.

"I'm still not impressed," Bancroft replied.

"You better bring an army if you're going after Frances Neagley," Dixon said.

Bancroft raised his eyebrows at her.

"Oh, we don't have an army," he said. "We've got something even better."

Chapter 27

Neagley drove.

Cooper sat in the front passenger seat, a nod to his immense bulk.

O'Donnell sat behind Neagley; Chavez, who needed the least amount of leg room, sat behind Cooper. He was working on a laptop connected to a wireless signal put out by his cell phone.

"Check your email, Chavez," Neagley said. "My researcher back in Chicago found some stuff on Sanzer and I had her send it to you."

"Got it. I found some stuff out on my own, too."

"Well, we've got a few hours to kill, so let's hear what you've got."

"Okay," Chavez began. "Sanzer was started by a man named Pribbenow. Dr. Scott Pribbenow. Ivy League degrees with a focus on molecular biology. Wrote a few papers, formed Sanzer, and then, to be honest, not a lot of information after that."

"That doesn't make sense. If they're cheating on their taxes to the tune of a half billion dollars, surely they're doing something," O'Donnell said. "How could his information trail run dry?"

"What about the name Yost mentioned? Adria?" Cooper asked. "I thought it was a person, but maybe it's a drug, made by Sanzer?"

"That makes sense," Neagley added. "Maybe Dixon found a small accounting error in the Adria division of Sanzer."

"It sounds like something you'd take for insomnia or a sleep disorder," Cooper offered.

"Nope," Chavez said, digging through his search results. "Nothing about any drugs made by Sanzer. Pribbenow's history seems to drop off a few years ago. No mention of a drug named Adria, either."

He tapped on his keyboard. "Your gal in Chicago searched Adria, too and didn't find anything. No such drug known."

"What the hell was Yost talking about then?"

"He was scared," O'Donnell said. "Not making sense. That whole thing about kneecapping someone. It was just weird."

"Maybe not," Chavez said. He was looking at his laptop.

"I fed Adria into my hacking systems and I got a hit. And it has nothing to do with drugs."

"What then?" Neagley asked.

"Not Adria, exactly. But I got a hit on DRIA. It's an acronym."

"What's it stand for?"

"Advanced Defense Research and Innovation Applications."

"What the hell kind of gibberish is that?" Cooper asked.

"Who would name their company that?" O'Donnell asked.

"It's not a company."

"Then what is it?"

"A branch of the government."

"Oh, the alphabet soup name makes perfect sense then. That's classic government-speak," Cooper said.

"What branch?" Neagley asked. "I've never heard of it."

"Yeah," Chavez said. "Apparently, it's a small department."

"Within what?"

"The Department of Defense."

Chapter 28

Neagley guided the black sedan to the freeway exit and took it, then followed directions to an industrial park about forty minutes southwest of DC. It was a mostly deserted area, too far from DC to benefit from the tax base, and not attractive enough for any business investment. It looked like the kind of place that would appear no different in thirty years.

"You sure this is the right address?" Cooper asked.

"Yeah, I'm sure," Chavez answered. "I've never been to the headquarters of a pharmaceutical company, so I've got nothing to compare it to, but this doesn't look like what I thought it would."

"Maybe this is the factory where they make the crap," O'Donnell said. "Toxic fumes or something. They need a place devoid of people, and they sure found it."

"I thought all the drug factories were overseas somewhere," Coop replied. "You know, India. Bangladesh. Puerto Rico."

"Used to be Puerto Rico then they changed the tax code and everyone left," Chavez said. "That's why PR went bankrupt."

Neagley studied the terrain. They were at the intersection of a two-lane road that ran parallel to the warehouses and a surface street they'd followed from the freeway. It was like a dead end of sorts. She saw no signs of a gate or an entrance.

"Let's follow this industrial road, maybe there's a gate somewhere," O'Donnell suggested.

Neagley put the car in gear and turned right.

The sky was overcast, a looming sheet of gray with the hint of rain on the horizon. They followed the road and it made a gentle curve, exposing more structures made of aluminum siding and not much else.

"There," O'Donnell said.

Ahead, the fence that separated the road from the buildings opened up into a driveway.

Neagley drove ahead.

There was a little guardhouse and it was clearly unoccupied. The door and windows were wide open, no one inside.

The chain-link gate remained closed. Behind it was another smaller warehouse, with a double set of glass doors and three parking spaces. If there was an office in the place, that was it.

Nowhere did she see any signs bearing the name "Sanzer."

Movement reflected in the rearview mirror caught her eye.

She glanced up and as automatic rifle fire erupted behind them, she shouted, "Down!"

Chapter 29

Ace stood in the home where Dr. Pribbenow had been cowering.

He knew this because he could literally smell the fear.

But he was too late. Pribbenow was gone, along with his security detail. His old pals.

Ace could tell the man had been surrounded by an entire phalanx of armed guards. There had probably been at least half a dozen of them. Some outside, others in.

He had just missed them, he knew that.

Probably just by an hour or two. There was still the lingering scent of coffee in the air, along with gun oil and from the doctor, fear. That odor was strongest in the man's home office, where a computer had been. The machine was gone, and in its place a fine outline made of dust that clearly showed where it had been positioned.

Ace pictured the good doctor sitting behind the desk, furiously trying to come up with a solution to the very problem he had created…and failing.

It was why the man had hidden here. It was where he was most comfortable. He had probably imagined dying here, at his desk.

The idea had probably given him comfort.

Ace's jaw bulged and his hands clenched.

There'd be nothing comforting about what he intended to do to the doctor.

He would kill him, as quickly and brutally as possible.

Chapter 30

Neagley didn't think. She acted on instinct.

Her eyes had taken in the chain-link gate and noted there was no padlock. It was secured only by a hinge linked to an electric motor somewhere.

She stomped on the accelerator and the big black car hit the gate securely. The frame must have held because the car jumped, something snapped and there was a horrible screeching sound that combined with the gunfire to sound like the opening fusillade in a small war.

The black sedan plowed over the mesh wire of the gate and then they were through.

Neagley peeked over the dash and saw there was nowhere to go. The drive ended in a circle that fed vehicles right back to the gate. She slammed on the brakes and reefed the wheel to the left, sending the car into a slide.

Dead Men Walking (Jack Reacher's Special Investigators)

Bullets crashed into the vehicle. Metal popped and glass shattered.

The car came to rest broadside from the gate and the four of them all moved as one, sliding out of the far doors and coming to rest behind the vehicle as bullets continued to crash into the sedan.

"Jesus – where did that come from?" Chavez shouted.

"Anyone hit?" Neagley asked.

"Dinged on the leg, no big deal," Cooper said. A deep gash ran across his enormous thigh. Neagley could see the dark red flesh inside.

"They knew we were coming," O'Donnell said.

With her Glock in hand, Neagley ducked around the corner of the car and glanced toward the gate.

What she saw shocked her.

Six men. All armed.

Walking toward them.

Without bulletproof vests. Overconfident? Or did they think everyone was dead?

She glanced over at Chavez, O'Donnell and Coop.

"Time to knock 'em down," she said.

They rose as one and began to fire.

Chapter 31

Neagley chose to target the attacker on her right, knowing her team instinctively would do the same respective to their position. Chavez would shoot the one on the far left, Cooper and O'Donnell would fire at the remaining gunmen in the middle.

If there were any survivors, they would mop them up together.

With her favorite pistol in hand, Neagley shot a three-round burst into the chest of the man coming directly toward her.

The man made no evasive moves. Didn't try to duck or take cover. His shirt, a black tactical vest, erupted as the big bullets tore through. The rounds were .45 ACP; a big, brutal round that could cause serious damage. One was enough to demolish a man's chest cavity. Three would cause immense and immediate evisceration.

Neagley watched as the man took her rounds in the chest. She waited for him to fall.

He didn't.

Instead, he staggered briefly, then seemed to gather himself and raised his rifle.

Neagley ducked back as the bullets crashed into the metal of the car. When the firing stopped, she wheeled again, took aim, and shot at the man's pelvis. Break a man's pelvis and he won't walk for three months.

She fired again and the man stumbled. He fell to the side. Some of his comrades were down in the dirt, too.

Neagley took the time to reload. She glanced down at her team next to her. They were all reloading as well. No one other than Cooper had been hit.

Neagley rammed home her fresh ammo, and spun back into her firing position. She stood and took aim.

And then she saw something that shocked her even more.

The fallen soldiers had all gotten to their feet.

Not only did they not appear to be injured, they were doing something that horrified Neagley even more.

They were smiling.

Chapter 32

Neagley didn't hesitate. She dove into the vehicle, keyed the engine, heard the sound of bullets crashing all around her. If she didn't get them out of there, they would all be dead in a matter of minutes. She had no time to think through what she'd seen. Hidden body armor? Kevlar clothing?

It just didn't make sense.

And there wasn't time to contemplate.

There was no need to communicate the plan – they had all seen the men get up from their gunshot wounds apparently unhurt. They didn't need to be told they were doomed if they stayed and tried to keep up a firefight against men who were immune to their weapons.

The car groaned to one side and Neagley knew Cooper was in. O'Donnell was next to her and she heard Chavez yell, "Go!"

She gunned the car and it careened forward. Glass shattered all around her and something bit into the side of her face. O'Donnell took a round in the shoulder and it drove him against the side of the car. Blood was everywhere.

Neagley floored the accelerator and the car fishtailed into position. She eased off the gas and the car shot forward.

It plowed into one of the gunmen, and he flipped up over the hood into the windshield and over the top of the vehicle.

Neagley saw the gate ahead and the opening where she'd plowed through the heart of the fence. Whatever had hit her in the face had opened cuts, because blood was streaming into her eyes. It was hard to see where she was going but she absolutely could not slow down.

She aimed the big sedan straight ahead and thumped over the lower rail of the gate and then they were out. Neagley once again stomped the accelerator, and mercifully the engine appeared undamaged because the sedan shot ahead. She did the best she could to steer, felt the car veer off the road and fought it back between the lines.

She heard engines rev behind her but the gunshots had stopped.

"What the hell was that?" Cooper boomed.

Neagley flew down the road, took a left onto the service road toward the freeway and saw no one behind her. She used her sleeve to wipe the blood from her face.

"Dave, are you okay?" she asked O'Donnell. He leaned forward and she saw the bullet had gone through his shoulder and out his back, just above the shoulder blade. It was messy and bloody, but he would survive.

"Just dandy," O'Donnell replied.

"Anyone else hit?"

"We're good," Chavez said. "Can you actually see to drive?"

Her mind tried to reconcile what she'd just witnessed, but it couldn't.

Neagley ignored his question.

All she could think about at that moment was Karla Dixon.

Chapter 33

Dixon couldn't take her eyes off the man.

He was small, maybe 5'7" or so, thin, bowed shoulders, a big forehead, and a mop of hair that he couldn't seem to keep in place.

What made his size so comical were the men surrounding him. Absolute monsters. All of them well over six feet, at least 250 pounds or more. It was like looking at six Jack Reachers.

And then you had Bancroft who, even though he wasn't a small man, had suddenly diminished in size.

They were huddled together at the back of a big room that appeared to be their center of operations. Dixon had been brought from the interrogation room to here. It looked like final decisions were being made.

Bancroft was in charge, that much was certain.

The little man was off to the side. Closer to Dixon. Sort of listening, but mostly looking afraid of what he might hear.

Dixon caught his eye.

"You're Pribbenow?" she asked.

The little man glanced over toward Bancroft and the soldiers, saw they weren't really watching him, and nodded.

"Yeah."

"How does it feel to have started this whole mess?"

"I never intended to. I'm a scientist."

"Sorry, doesn't let you off the hook."

Bancroft glanced their way, saw them talking but his expression said it didn't matter. In Dixon's mind, that wasn't a good sign.

"Who are you? How did you get mixed up in this?" Pribbenow asked.

"Your owner's bookkeeping got a little creative," Dixon said. "When I pointed it out, all hell broke loose."

"Sanzer?" Pribbenow asked.

"Yes."

"Just a shell company," the little man said. "A front for DRIA."

"I was just starting to figure that out when they grabbed me."

Pribbenow nodded. "They have spies everywhere. A huge budget."

From somewhere down the hall, several explosions rattled the building.

Pribbenow actually screamed.

Rifle fire followed as Bancroft and the soldiers took up position near the door. Two of them stood on each side of Pribbenow, who looked up at Dixon.

"We're all going to die," he said.

"Yeah, but why?" Dixon asked. She was strangely calm.

Pribbenow had started to cry.

Snot ran down his nose and then he finally spoke.

"*He's here.*"

Chapter 34

Neagley saw the entrance to the freeway up ahead.

She weighed her options then threw the battered vehicle into a sharp left turn. She jumped the cement median, and bounced over the curb back onto the road going toward the warehouse.

"What's the plan, Neagley?" Coop asked.

"Dixon's back there somewhere. We can't leave her."

She drove forward and no one argued.

O'Donnell spoke. "You know, as I watched those robots or whatever they hell they were get back up, I kept thinking about DRIA and how it's actually a part of the Department of Defense."

"Yeah, now we know that for sure," Coop said. "Those superhuman soldiers back there were part of DRIA for sure."

"I know. But Yost mentioned DRIA, and then he also talked about kneecapping someone. But you know what the military loves more than big budgets?"

"Acronyms," Neagley said.

"Exactly," O'Donnell replied. "It's not kneecap. It's NECAP."

Chavez retrieved his dented and mangled laptop from the floor of the car. It was a miracle it still worked, but it did. He punched in some information.

"Holy shit," he said. "NECAP stands for Nanoengineered Advanced Combat Personnel."

"What the hell does that mean?" Coop asked. "What's a nano?"

"Nanoengineering, or nanomedicine, more likely, is science on a molecular level," Neagley said. "The military's been screwing around with it for years. Now those freaks back there are starting to make sense."

"Wait," O'Donnell said. "Weren't we talking about the guy who started Sanzer? A Dr. Pribbenow? Didn't it say somewhere he was a molecular biologist?"

"He's working for the Department of Defensc," Chavez said.

"Yeah, but what does nanomedicine have to do with those dudes back there?"

"The theory was that nanomedicine could

eventually alter a human being at the molecular level," Neagley said. "It can give them better eyesight, sense of smell, superhuman strength, instant tissue repair. It was all just a wild theory no one actually thought was possible."

"Well, I'm a believer now that I saw it firsthand. The shit works," Cooper said.

"Yeah. Dixon must have found some accounting anomaly in a pharmaceutical company tied to Sanzer and she worked her way backward. Ran into NECAP and some idiots at Defense who weren't going to let a little forensic accountant spoil their big plans."

"That's what the half billion dollars is for," O'Donnell said. "The DOD is illegally funding this company and Dixon somehow found out."

Silence settled in the car.

Neagley drove on, the sound of broken pieces of metal dragging along the road and wind whistling through the broken windows gave the moment a surreal quality.

"How are we going to beat these guys?" O'Donnell asked.

Neagley smiled. "I don't know, but they are dead men walking."

Chapter 35

It was the most epic gun battle Dixon had ever seen.

A huge man filled the doorway from out of nowhere and began firing. He had an enormous weapon in his hands. Dixon knew what it was: an M134 Minigun. It had six barrels and fired like an old-style Gatling gun. It shot monstrous 7.62 x 51mm rounds – thousands of them per minute.

As she watched, the man leveled the gun at Bancroft's men and began firing. What happened next was straight out of a horror movie. The soldiers were literally blown apart. Chunks of flesh, parts of arms and legs, even a head, flew apart in a monstrous vapor of red blood.

Pribbenow was screaming.

Dixon had fallen to the floor and belly crawled as far away as she could.

The men with Bancroft were destroyed. Only one was still alive. He somehow staggered to his feet and fired back at the man with the Minigun.

Bancroft was taking cover behind a steel desk as the guns blazed.

Dixon heard the rotary-style machine gun go empty. She saw the big man hurl the weapon aside and bring his rifle to bear. He and Bancroft's remaining soldier poured bullets into each other.

To Dixon's astonishment, they seemed to have no effect.

It was only a matter of time before someone ran out of ammunition.

Dixon didn't understand what she was seeing. Bancroft's man should have been dead, and she'd seen the lone gunman at the door take bullets to the chest as well. In fact, his shirt was torn and she saw a tattoo that read ACE.

One of the men on the ground who'd had his arm blown and suffered multiple gunshots all over his body, was also getting to his feet.

Impossible, Dixon thought.

Pribbenow saw her and his eyes were bright. He was terrified and Dixon suddenly realized, crazy.

"Advanced Combat Engincered. Ace. My masterpiece."

There was a lull in the gunfire as the soldiers reloaded.

"Your creation. So why does he want to kill you?"

Pribbenow pulled a device smaller than a cell phone from his pocket. It had a single button protruding from the slim, silver case.

"He was the only one smart enough to figure this out."

His hands were shaking.

"What is it?" Dixon asked.

"It sends a signal that turns on a gene inside them that will instantly stop their hearts. Instantaneous death. Ace 1 knows I can kill him at any time. But it will kill them all. I can't differentiate between any of them. That's why I—"

Bullets ripped up the floor next to Pribbenow and then they worked sideways. Flesh was torn from his back as machine gun fire blew apart his chest cavity and tore his head apart. A river of blood ran out from beneath him.

The control device flew from his grasp and slid across the floor to Dixon.

She scooped it up.

Everyone in the room had stopped and was looking at her.

Ace had stopped firing into Bancroft's man and had turned his gun on Pribbenow. Now, he was looking at her, raising his rifle.

Bancroft's man was still firing into Ace, but the bullets were simply having no effect.

Dixon's thumb found the button.

"No!" Bancroft yelled. He got to his feet, started to run toward Dixon and raised his pistol toward her.

She pressed the button.

Dixon watched the huge man fall to the ground and she dove for the nearest one who had just done the same. She pried his pistol from his hip and rolled onto her back just as Bancroft slid to a stop. Dixon saw his finger tighten on the trigger.

She fired, a double tap and both bullets entered Bancroft's forehead within milliseconds of each other.

He was knocked backward and landed on the floor, his expensive watch cracked on the cement.

The room was silent then and filled with the odor of spent ammunition, blood and death.

"Nice shot, Karla," Neagley said as she stepped into the room, her Glock held out in front of her.

Dixon saw the blood all over her face. O'Donnell, Cooper and Chavez fanned out behind her. They were wounded, but looked to be all in one piece.

She let go of the gun and the metal device.

"You got my 1030," she said.

Neagley nodded. "Roger that."

Chapter 36

Neagley sat in the BMW, the big V12 idling, its power bubbling just beneath the surface. She sat in the parking lot just north of Chicago and studied the front of the building.

Lake Shore Animal Shelter.

She knew she was stalling.

After they'd rescued Dixon and been interviewed by all kinds of law enforcement, including the FBI, medical care had been required. Neagley had received some stitches on the side of her neck. O'Donnell had surgery to repair a broken shoulder blade. And Cooper had his thigh stitched up.

Only Chavez and Dixon had escaped relatively unscathed.

Once they were able, they spent a couple nights together, drinking, reminiscing about good times in the Army, catching up. They were like a family and totally at ease with each other.

It had made Neagley happy and sad at the same time.

Because she knew she would be going home. To an empty house.

Which is why she let out a deep breath and shut off the BMW. She pocketed the keys and walked up to the front of the animal shelter and opened the door.

Inside, she was shown around the place and saw the animals available for adoption.

One of them was a big hound. Muscular. Quiet. Intelligent. The shelter worker said he'd been neglected and possibly abused. They had all fallen in love with him because he gave them no trouble. He just seemed sad, as if he'd never known what it was like to be happy.

"I'll take him," Neagley said.

She went up to the front office and filled out the required paperwork.

Being who she was, Neagley had already bought a leash and collar. She had dog food and bowls ready at the house. It had been her way of postponing the decision during the months she had come and parked in the lot, just staring at the entrance. Never working up the nerve to actually come inside.

Until now.

As she and her hound prepared to leave the shelter, the worker stopped her.

"What do you think you'll call him?" she asked.

Neagley smiled.

"Reacher."

BUY THE NEXT BOOK IN THE SERIES!

CLICK HERE TO BUY BOOK TWO NOW!

A USA TODAY
BESTSELLING BOOK

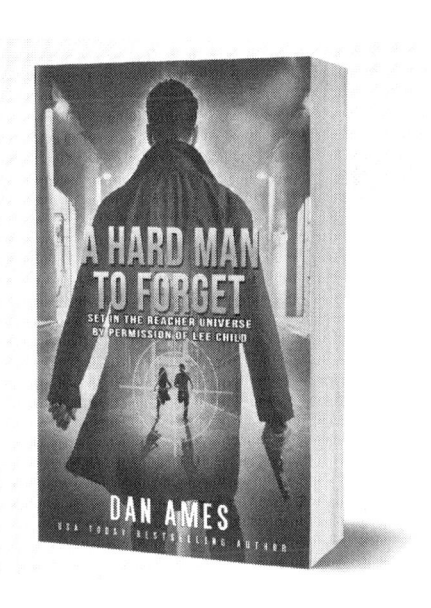

Book One in The JACK REACHER Cases

CLICK HERE TO BUY NOW

A Fast-Paced Action-Packed Thriller Series

CLICK HERE TO BUY

An Award-Winning
Bestselling Mystery Series

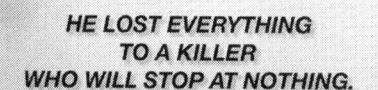

Buy DEAD WOOD, the first John Rockne Mystery.

CLICK HERE TO BUY

"Fast-paced, engaging, original."
-NYTimes bestselling author Thomas Perry

About the Author

Dan Ames is a USA TODAY Bestselling Author, Amazon Kindle #1 bestseller and winner of the Independent Book Award for Crime Fiction.

www.authordanames.com
Dan@authordanames.com

Also by Dan Ames

THE JACK REACHER CASES

The JACK REACHER Cases #1 (A Hard Man To Forget)

The JACK REACHER Cases #2 (The Right Man For Revenge)

The JACK REACHER Cases #3 (A Man Made For Killing)

The JACK REACHER Cases #4 (The Last Man To Murder)

The JACK REACHER Cases #5 (The Man With No Mercy)

The JACK REACHER Cases #6 (A Man Out For Blood)

The JACK REACHER Cases #7 (A Man Beyond The Law)

The JACK REACHER Cases #8 (The Man Who Walks Away)

The JACK REACHER Cases (The Man Who Strikes Fear)

The JACK REACHER Cases (The Man Who Stands Tall)

The JACK REACHER Cases (The Man Who Works Alone)

The Jack Reacher Cases (A Man Built For Justice)

The JACK REACHER Cases #13 (A Man Born for Battle)

The JACK REACHER Cases #14 (The Perfect Man for Payback)

The JACK REACHER Cases #15 (The Man Whose Aim Is True)

The JACK REACHER Cases #16 (The Man Who Dies Here)

The JACK REACHER Cases #17 (The Man With Nothing To Lose)

The JACK REACHER Cases #18 (The Man Who Never Goes Back)

The JACK REACHER Cases #19 (The Man From The Shadows)

The JACK REACHER CASES #20 (The Man Behind The Gun)

JACK REACHER'S SPECIAL INVESTIGATORS

BOOK ONE: DEAD MEN WALKING

BOOK TWO: GAME OVER

BOOK THREE: LIGHTS OUT

BOOK FOUR: NEVER FORGIVE, NEVER FORGET

BOOK FIVE: HIT THEM FAST, HIT THEM HARD

BOOK SIX: FINISH THE FIGHT

THE JOHN ROCKNE MYSTERIES

DEAD WOOD (John Rockne Mystery #1)
HARD ROCK (John Rockne Mystery #2)
COLD JADE (John Rockne Mystery #3)
LONG SHOT (John Rockne Mystery #4)
EASY PREY (John Rockne Mystery #5)
BODY BLOW (John Rockne Mystery #6)

THE WADE CARVER THRILLERS

MOLLY (Wade Carver Thriller #1)

SUGAR (Wade Carver Thriller #2)

ANGEL (Wade Carver Thriller #3)

THE WALLACE MACK THRILLERS

THE KILLING LEAGUE (Wallace Mack Thriller #1)

THE MURDER STORE (Wallace Mack Thriller #2)

FINDERS KILLERS (Wallace Mack Thriller #3)

THE MARY COOPER MYSTERIES

DEATH BY SARCASM (Mary Cooper Mystery #1)

MURDER WITH SARCASTIC INTENT (Mary Cooper Mystery #2)

GROSS SARCASTIC HOMICIDE (Mary Cooper Mystery #3)

THE CIRCUIT RIDER (WESTERNS)

THE CIRCUIT RIDER (Circuit Rider #1)
KILLER'S DRAW (Circuit Rider #2)

THE RAY MITCHELL THRILLERS

THE RECRUITER

KILLING THE RAT

HEAD SHOT

STANDALONE THRILLERS:

KILLER GROOVE (Rockne & Cooper Mystery #1)

BEER MONEY (Burr Ashland Mystery #1)

TO FIND A MOUNTAIN (A WWII Thriller)

BOX SETS:

AMES TO KILL

GROSSE POINTE PULP

GROSSE POINTE PULP 2

TOTAL SARCASM

WALLACE MACK THRILLER COLLECTION

SHORT STORIES:

THE GARBAGE COLLECTOR

BULLET RIVER

SCHOOL GIRL

HANGING CURVE

SCALE OF JUSTICE

Free Books And More

Would you like a FREE copy of my story BULLET RIVER and the chance to win a free Kindle?

Then sign up for the DAN AMES BOOK CLUB:

For special offers and new releases, sign up here

A USA TODAY BESTSELLING AUTHOR

GAME OVER

SET IN THE REACHER UNIVERSE
BY PERMISSION OF LEE CHILD

DAN AMES

A USA TODAY BESTSELLING BOOK

Book One in The JACK REACHER Cases

CLICK HERE TO BUY NOW

Praise for Dan Ames

"Fast-paced, engaging, original."
> New York TIMES BESTSELLING AUTHOR Thomas Perry

"Ames is a sensation among readers who love fast-paced thrillers."
> MYSTERY TRIBUNE

"Cuts like a knife."
> Savannah Morning News

"Furiously paced. Great action."
> New York TIMES BESTSELLING AUTHOR Ben Lieberman

Free Books And More

Would you like a FREE copy of my story BULLET RIVER and the chance to win a free Kindle?

Then sign up for the DAN AMES BOOK CLUB:

For special offers and new releases, sign up here

GAME OVER

Jack Reacher's Special Investigators #2

by

Dan Ames

Chapter 1

Before most of them died, there was a heated debate over regional barbecue. Private Jeremy Walker of a small town near Lockhart, Texas, was adamant the best barbecue didn't use sauce, but rather, dry rubs.

"Texas is number one for barbecue, hands down," he said. "Anyone else say otherwise, ya'll full of shit."

"Hold on, boy," Private Amos Greene of Rocky Mount, North Carolina, countered. "You ever had Carolina pulled pork made with a mop sauce?"

"Why the hell I want anything made with a mop?" Walker replied.

"Mop *sauce*," Greene said. "Vinegar-based with spices and secret ingredients. No better pulled pork in the world. Carolina barbecue is the world's best, no doubt about it."

Second Lieutenant Gutierrez weighed in. "Both of you need to pipe down and pay attention." He scanned the surrounding line of mountains, bathed in shadow, as the team descended into a narrow valley in northern Afghanistan. Gutierrez had a bad feeling, but then again, he usually did.

This was a bad operation and he knew it.

They were escorting a motley collection of opium traders along with a group of American civilian contractors under unofficial arrest for war crimes and a contingent of military police. The large American base near Mazar-i-Sharif was their destination, but they still had an hour to go.

This area was known to all as an insurgent hotbed. Lots of bad guys, heavily armed.

The convoy was a collection of Hummers and one mine sweeper. The rest were on foot. Gutierrez and his men had taken the point position. Tip of the spear, as they say.

"Besides," the Second Lieutenant born and raised near Memphis, Tennessee, added, "Memphis barbecue puts Texas, Carolina and Kansas City to shame. Doesn't matter if it's dry, wet or any and all in between. Why the hell you think they have the Barbecue World Championships every year in Memphis–"

GAME OVER (Jack Reacher's Special Investigators)

The first RPG came whistling in from above.

"Incoming!" someone yelled.

The round scored a direct hit on the first Humvee. The sound was deafening and a thick cloud of black smoke belched from the ruined vehicle as flames erupted. Men dove for cover amid more shouts and the first of many screams to come.

Machine gun fire poured in from above and Gutierrez's worst fears were realized. He'd argued against marching a convoy of this size down into and through a narrow valley. It was perfect terrain for an ambush. They'd given the enemy high ground and put themselves in the worst possible defensive position.

The enemy was now proving him right.

And then things became worse.

Machine gun fire poured in from the hills around them. To Gutierrez's trained ears, most of the fire was from AK-47s, the rifles favored by the Taliban and insurgents everywhere. It was a low-quality gun, difficult to shoot accurately but parts were ubiquitous and should a round find its target, it could cause severe and deadly damage.

The AKs didn't bother Gutierrez, however.

What caught his ear and filled his stomach with an icy sense of dread was the sound of a much heavier machine gun. It was the infamous DShK machine gun. It fired a 12.7 x 108mm cartridge that was nearly six inches long and could literally blow a man apart.

Gutierrez entered the fog of war: around him smoke billowed, bullets tore into the ground and everywhere, men were screaming.

Behind him, he saw the convoy literally disintegrate before his eyes as bullets, RPGs and mortar rounds poured into their midst.

Yea though I walk through the valley of the shadow of death, he thought, having recited the prayer hundreds of times in the heat of battle.

He shouted into his headset for his comms team to relay the coordinates and ask for air support.

Unfortunately, Gutierrez never got the chance to hear the reply.

A mortar screamed in from above and exploded less than a foot from the native Tennessean. There was a brief flash of white and then Gutierrez's body was instantly reduced to a burnt and smoking geyser of blood, bone and tissue.

His death was only the beginning.

Chapter 2

The Hazeltines lived in a 15,000-square-foot sprawling mansion in a wealthy suburb outside Washington, DC. It was the kind of home befitting two surgeons. Dr. Philip Hazeltine was an orthopedic surgeon while his wife Annette Hazeltine was an emergency room surgeon.

Current private investigator and former Army military policeman Dave O'Donnell drove his Jeep Grand Cherokee SUV up the sprawling driveway where he parked, got out of the vehicle and rang the bell on the massive, mahogany front door.

Dave was built like a greyhound: tall, sinewy and taut with muscle. He was like a coiled spring with a limitless supply of encrgy on hand. He was dressed in his usual style: a neat, modern suit with an athletic cut.

A security camera looked down at him from an alcove above the door.

Moments later the huge door creaked open on its wrought iron hinges and revealed the family's assistant. She was of Spanish descent and her name was Gloria. Dave had met her once before. She smiled and said, "Please come in, the doctor is expecting you."

Dave followed her inside as she shut the door behind them. The foyer was cavernous, the floor was made of Italian marble, the walls held towering oil paintings and from the ceiling hung a glittering chandelier.

It was the kind of entrance befitting two highly compensated and well-regarded physicians.

Off to Dave's right was a butler's pantry and beyond that an enormous professional kitchen. To his left was a formal dining room that branched out in two directions to a sunroom and a family room. Beyond the foyer was a study lined with bookshelves and more paintings.

Straight ahead was a hallway that led to the back of the house where a wall of glass sliding doors revealed an outdoor living space home to an Olympic-size swimming pool. Gloria gestured toward the sliding doors and Dave walked through them and stepped out onto the concrete pool deck.

It was an expansive space that included an

outdoor dining area under a pergola as well as a series of chaise lounge chairs made of teak with white cushions. A line of neatly pruned boxwood shrubs surrounded the area and several large turquoise vases held plants that looked like miniature palm trees.

To the left was another sitting area facing an outdoor fireplace. To the right was a gourmet outdoor kitchen complete with one of the largest gas grills Dave had ever seen along with a counter, sink and refrigerator.

Philip Hazeltine sat on a teak bench next to the pool. He was a large man, in his late fifties with a tanned, muscular body that spoke to hours in the home gym lifting weights. Along with a possible bevy of steroids and supplements.

He had on a coral-colored swimming suit and his dark hair was slicked back. A towel was draped over one of his massive shoulders.

Philip was not Dave's client. Rebecca Hazeltine, the daughter of Philip and Annette, had hired Dave because her mother had been missing for several weeks and she was suspicious. Rebecca said her dad could be very controlling.

According to Rebecca, Annette had told her daughter she was going to a conference in Miami but Dave's investigative work showed that while she had, in fact, registered for the conference, she had never arrived.

Working backwards, Dave was also able to confirm that Annette had not boarded the flight she'd booked in order to attend the conference.

Philip said the last time he'd seen his wife was when she was leaving for the airport.

Now, Dave stood before Philip and the two were a study in contrast. While Philip was all relaxed bulk and artificial nutrients primed by weight machines, Dave O'Donnell was lean intensity. His suit failed to reveal a set of brass knuckles and zip ties in one pocket and a switchblade knife in the other. They were tools of the trade from his Army days when he served under Jack Reacher. They were habits he had never broken.

"Hey Dave, what's the good word?" Philip asked. He grinned, revealing a set of brilliant white teeth that seemed to radiate out from the surrounding tanned skin of his face. It reminded Dave of a wolf baring its teeth against an implied threat.

"The word is disappointment," Dave replied. "Still no word from Annette?"

"No, sir." Philip showed no emotion, one way or the other.

Dave hesitated. Over the years as both an Army investigator and a private detective he had learned to trust his instincts and at the moment something was bothering him.

Something was off.

He let the silence linger and forced his awareness to roam. What was it? What was bothering him?

Philip was the same as always: tan, muscular and confident.

Gloria had been the same.

The house had been the same.

And then he stopped himself.

No, that wasn't right. The house wasn't exactly the same. Something right here was different, he realized.

"Have a seat, Dave," Philip said. He beamed at Dave, raised a meaty hand toward a cement bench opposite the teak seating area.

Dave looked at the bench and realized he had never noticed it before. It had a horizontal base that was textured. Above that was the seating platform and it was at least three feet thick. It was a slightly different color than the base and it was smooth.

Nothing wrong with that. It made sense the two pieces would be different. But the way it was built struck Dave as odd. Who wants to sit on a roughly textured cement seat wearing a swimming suit? Uncomfortable, to say the least.

Dave also realized Philip was studying him with a smile on his face. Almost like he was gloating. Dave walked over to the bench and looked at it. He touched its surface. There was a little bit of cement dust and mortar pieces behind the bench between it and the wall.

Dave's back straightened as he heard the whisper of movement behind him. It was the very gentle scrape of bare feet on the pool deck. He turned and his hand automatically slipped into the set of brass knuckles in his pocket.

Corkscrewing his body, Dave turned and took it all in before him: Philip like a bull charging him, his face no longer bearing a smile but a ferocious snarl, murder in his eyes. Dave's tightly coiled body unleashed and threw an uppercut that was perfectly timed.

It was a beautifully thrown and delivered punch that carried a fierce amount of energy unleashed by Dave's own taut and powerful body. He drove his fist home using what Jack Reacher used to call the cigarette punch, an old standard among military policemen.

It was called that because you offer the guy you're trying to arrest a cigarette and he takes it and lifts it to his lips and opens his mouth maybe three quarters of an inch. Whereupon you time it just right and land a huge uppercut under his chin. It slams his mouth shut and breaks his jaw and busts his teeth and maybe he bites off his tongue.

Thank you and good night.

Dave didn't need to offer Philip a cigarette

because his mouth was already partly open in anticipation. Like a wild animal about to pounce.

The punch caught the doctor on the bottom of the chin. Philip's jaw snapped shut with such force that it broke a handful of his veneered teeth that exploded from his mouth and dropped to the pool deck like a handful of spare change.

Dave danced to the side as Philip swayed on his feet. Dave threw a wicked right cross that caught Philip on the side of the jaw and the bigger man's body crashed forward face first onto the pool deck.

Dave used his foot to turn Philip's face toward him.

Philip's eyes had rolled back into his head and his body stiffened. He was out.

Game over, Dave thought.

He immediately kneeled on Philip's back, pulled out the zip tie and bound the doctor's hands behind him. He took out his phone and dialed 911.

When the dispatcher answered, Dave said he needed detectives and crime scene techs. He then gave her the Hazeltines address.

He glanced over at the cement bench and added, "I also believe I've found the body of Annette Hazeltine."

Chapter 3

Newsome and Steiner sat in the front seats of the van. Newsome drove while Steiner was half-turned in her seat, looking back at the third person in the van.

He was on the floor, his hands and feet bound, a strip of duct tape across his mouth. A few cardboard boxes were next to him, stuffed with papers and file folders. Jutting out from the top of one of the boxes was a ten-year-old computer.

"Persistence might make you a good investigator, Joe," Steiner said to the man on the floor. "But it can get you killed too, if you're not careful."

"And you weren't careful," Newsome added. He looked in the rearview mirror, sat up straighter so he could see the man on the floor.

"Joe Reynolds," Steiner continued. "Private investigator. Former military policeman. Divorced father of one. Killed for not knowing when to back the hell out. Hell of a legacy," she said.

She turned and faced the front. "Turn here," she instructed Newsome.

He guided the van to the intersection and turned right. Eventually, Steiner's navigation had them arriving at an industrial yard with a broken gate and junked cars everywhere. The rusted-out vehicles were not parked in any kind of organization, rather it appeared as if they'd been dropped from the sky and remained where they landed.

"Go back there," Steiner said, gesturing with her chin toward the rear of the salvage yard.

Newsome drove the van behind a large piece of equipment that might have been a car carrier in its previous life. Now, it was a hulk of rusted industrial sculpture.

He parked and Steiner went to the back of the van. She opened the rear doors, pulled out a bag with gloves, booties and hospital scrubs. Newsome joined her and together they quickly dressed in the medical scrubs.

Once she was geared up, Steiner grabbed a three-foot reciprocating saw with a long, jagged blade on the end.

"Grab that jug," she told Newsome.

Each of them grabbed ahold of Reynolds and pulled him from the van. Together, they dragged him around behind the remains of the carrier where a large metal basin with a drain had been buried in the ground. Steiner figured it was an illegal way to get rid of unwanted gasoline and oil, or hazardous waste that would be too expensive for an operation like this to dispose of legally.

Reynolds' eyes were large and he looked at the tool in Steiner's hands.

"Cordless," she said, holding up the saw, a gleam in her eye. "Medical-grade blade. I could cut down trees with this son of a bitch."

Newsome knew how much Steiner enjoyed this kind of thing. Torture especially seemed to arouse her in unpredictable ways.

But they were in a hurry.

So he pulled out a pistol, pressed it to Reynolds' temple and pulled the trigger.

They waited a moment and after she gave him a frustrated glance that meant she clearly felt he'd deprived her of some serious entertainment, Steiner turned back to the task at hand. She quickly and methodically cut off the man's fingers, hands and toes. She worked her way to the bigger joints and severed more body parts, tossing them all down into the oversized drain.

"Okay, time for you to do some dentistry," she said to Newsome.

Newsome pulled the cap off the jug of battery acid and poured it all over Reynolds' face, and into his mouth.

"Use all of it, so not a single tooth will match his records," Steiner said. "It'll even burn through bone."

When they were done, they threw the jug and saw into the cab of a burned-out truck three hundred yards from the metal tub. They doused the equipment with gasoline and set it on fire.

They also tossed their scrubs into the flames along with the boxes of paperwork from the back of the van.

Once it had all burned, they got back into the van.

"You could have let me have some fun with him first," Steiner said. "We had plenty of time."

"No we don't," Newsome replied. "This will not go unnoticed."

Chapter 4

Special Investigations Inc. was headquartered in a second-story office on a mixed-use commercial street less than a half mile from the Capitol.

Dave O'Donnell had named his private investigative firm "Special Investigations" after his old team back in the Army. The crew of military police working under Jack Reacher had called themselves the special investigators and they had even come up with their own unofficial motto: *you do not mess with the special investigators.*

Now, Dave sat at his desk and read through the crime scene report from the Hazeltines. Over the years he had developed numerous contacts within the DC homicide department. He spoke their language, occasionally bought them drinks and traded war stories. Some of the young detectives looked up to him for the considerable police

GAME OVER (Jack Reacher's Special Investigators)

experience he offered, as well as his toughness and street smarts.

They even occasionally used Dave for "off the books" operations. For his help and support, he was routinely given access to a number of things like reports, license plate numbers, criminal database records and much more. All of it was done on the side, off the record.

When the cops and, eventually, the homicide detectives arrived at the Hazeltines, it didn't take long for them to request help processing a possible crime scene. The techs had arrived and done a scan of the cement bench using sonar and electromagnetic imaging. The test revealed a layer of organic matter near the bottom of the bench seat.

The careful dismantling of the cement – layer by layer – revealed stratification of multiple kinds of commercial cement, rocks, stones and even landscaping pebbles.

Finally, at the very bottom, they found the surgically dismantled remains of Annette Hazeltine.

Philip Hazeltine was arrested and charged with first-degree murder. Dave had already contacted his client, Rebecca, who understandably had burst into tears at the news her mom had indeed been murdered by her father. It was the worst possible outcome and the daughter was devastated.

The phone call was something Dave had dreaded, but he had suspected all along that Annette had been the victim of foul play. He'd gotten a bad vibe from Philip at the start and his instincts had turned out to be right.

It wasn't his first death notification but they were always extremely difficult. Dave had both the electronic and hard copy versions of the report and now he filed the paper copy in a folder and put that into a neatly organized file cabinet at the rear of his office.

The Special Investigations office consisted of two rooms: an entry/waiting room with seating and Dave's personal office. A door off of the waiting room opened up to Dave's office which held a seating area, his desk, a second table with another computer and an array of electronic equipment. There was a gun safe disguised as an ordinary cabinet and a second hidden safe behind a recessed panel which housed a fake thermostat.

Each member of Jack Reacher's Special Investigators unit had taken on special roles within the team. Although each was technically a homicide investigator they also possessed qualities and abilities utilized by the entire group.

Dave had always been the most organized and fastidious when it came to paperwork so that task had naturally fallen to him.

His office reflected that keen ability; there was

a place for everything and everything was in its place.

Dave worked the keyboard on his desktop computer and logged onto his bank's website and perused his business accounts. He checked to make sure they were all in balance and all of his subcontractors had been paid.

He frequently employed a variety of freelancers to handle such things as legal issues, surveillance, and photographers. For all of his computer work he hired Edgar Chavez, who lived in Venice, Florida, and had been a key member of the Special Investigators back in the Army. Chavez was a genius when it came to all things computer and web related.

Satisfied that his financial matters were taken care of Dave opened his email and went through them with the same kind of speed and precision for which he was legendary.

Until he came to the very last message.

It was from an email address that he was not familiar with. He knew spammers used email accounts all the time. As he understood, it was okay to open them but not to click on any links. The computer viruses were in the links and clicking activated them.

Dave opened the email.

It contained a message only two sentences long.

He read the message and recognized the name within it. An old friend from his days in the Army. A man who he'd respected and occasionally worked with side by side.

Dave read the message again.

He let out a slow breath.

It seemed Dave's day had begun with a homicide and now it was going to end with another one as well.

The message had been very clear.

Joe Reynolds is dead. I think he was murdered.

Chapter 5

"Still no word?" Newsome asked.

He caught sight of himself in the hotel room's mirror. He was tall and lean with broad shoulders, a shaved head and startling blue eyes that radiated intelligence and a default mode of aggression from across the room.

"Not a peep," Steiner said. She was the polar opposite of Newsome: a short, compact, solidly built woman with long black hair usually tied back into a tight ponytail. They both wore jeans with dark T-shirts and dark shoes.

They not only complemented each other appearance-wise but also in terms of capabilities. Newsome was a crack shot with a rifle or pistol. Steiner was a black belt in both jujitsu and aikido. She'd also trained exclusively in Krav Maga, the Israeli self-defense program.

Steiner was also the better communicator which is why she handled the computers and cell phones. Newsome was better with overall tactics and strategies and generally outlined plans and schedules.

But now the situation had taken an unexpected turn. A call they were waiting for didn't happen and a nuisance had become a crisis in need of an immediate and permanent solution.

They had been forced to respond.

"You do realize that killing Reynolds was only the beginning, right?" Newsome asked Steiner.

She closed the laptop.

"Yeah," she said. "We had no choice, but still, we may have kicked the hornet's nest."

Chapter 6

"Sit Reacher. Sit."

Frances Neagley's face remained impassive. She and the mixed breed hound stared at each other. Finally, his hindquarters lowered to the ground.

"Good boy," she said.

Neagley was amused by the dog and by the idea of naming a hound Reacher. It made sense. Reacher was a hound of sorts and when he was on the trail, he was relentless.

Neagley took a step back.

"Stay Reacher. Stay."

Neagley took another step back. The big hound's eyes were locked onto her. His mouth opened slightly and his pink tongue was barely visible as his breath quickened.

She narrowed her eyes at the dog and Reacher

cocked his head slightly to the side. His mouth snapped shut.

"Come here, Reacher!" Neagley slapped her thighs and the dog bolted from the floor, leaping four feet across the room. His paws scrambled for purchase on the hardwood floor and he raced into Neagley's arms.

She patted him and avoided his tongue as he tried to cover her face with slobbery kisses.

"Good boy," she said. "Good boy." Neagley had a treat in the palm of her hand and she fed it to him. She watched him eat it.

When he was done and was standing still looking at her for more instructions she said, "Take a bow, Reacher, take a bow."

The dog lowered his front paws and his shoulders halfway to the ground. And then popped back up.

"Good boy, Reacher!"

A treat materialized in Neagley's other hand and she fed it to the dog. She turned and walked into the kitchen while Reacher took a drink of water from his bowl.

Neagley lived in a mansion from the 1920s along Chicago's North Shore. It was a sprawling place and the neighborhood was one of the highest-income zip codes in the country.

Now, she looked out the window into the darkness. In the distance, she could make out the surface of Lake Michigan, illuminated by the full moon overhead.

Neagley grabbed her iPad from the kitchen counter and walked into her study. It was her favorite room in the house, just off the kitchen, and it was filled with books and comfortable leather furniture. Logs were burning and popping in the fireplace and Neagley plopped into the chair next to it. She put her feet up on the ottoman.

Reacher trotted in and flopped onto the rug in front of the roaring fire.

She opened her email and saw a message from a former colleague in the Army. The subject line was very simple: *did you see this?*

Neagley clicked on the link and read with growing interest and a sick feeling in her stomach about a brutal murder involving a former military policeman named Joe Reynolds.

She recognized the name.

Neagley let out a long, slow breath.

"Unacceptable," she said.

Chapter 7

Dave O'Donnell hung his head as he listened to the voice on the other end of the phone. The Army buddy who'd contacted Dave about Joe Reynolds didn't have much information, so Dave, being a relentless investigator, had done his homework. He'd tracked down the location of the crime, and worked backward from there until he knew which branch of the police had jurisdiction. And, more specifically, which homicide department.

He had discovered the name of the lead detective on the crime report, which he'd gotten by pulling a few strings.

"Turns out this Reynolds guy had one kid," the detective was saying. His name was Bozel. "A girl, who worried about him all the time. So Reynolds, being a private investigator and knowing all the tricks of the trade, had a GPS tracker inserted into his skin. Just to keep his daughter's anxiety in check. It was a tiny chip in the flesh just behind his armpit. His killer didn't notice."

"That's how you found the body?"

Bozel corrected Dave. "Not exactly."

"What do you mean?"

"We didn't find a body, only body parts. They cut him up into a bunch of pieces and poured acid down his mouth to prevent identification."

"But the chip survived."

"Sure did, because the torso wouldn't fit down the drain. And by then, his killers assumed no one would be able to figure out who it belonged to so they called it a day."

Dave thought about it. "I noticed you're using the plural. So more than one killer?"

"Almost positive, from the way the body was cut up and a few partial footprints," Bozel said. It sounded like he was reading from the same crime report Dave had. "Looks like more than one guy, but you never know."

Dave was tempted to ask Bozel for a full copy of the autopsy report as well, but it wasn't that kind of friendship; besides, he knew what he had to do.

"Mind if I pop up to Boston and buy you a beer?" Dave asked. The message was clear: I'd like more information but I'm not going to officially ask you for it. And certainly not over the phone.

"Ever known an Irish cop in Boston who turns down free booze?" Bozel replied.

Dave thanked him and said he'd shoot him a text when he arrived in town.

He sat back, lifted his long legs and put his feet on his desktop. He clasped his hands behind his head and remembered Joe Reynolds. A steady guy, Dave recalled. Low-key, quiet sense of humor but a dogged investigator. Really good at his craft. Not the first guy you'd turn to for help in a bar fight, but he could hold his own.

Dave was especially fond of Reynolds because the man had been older, had served as Dave's first mentor and was a big reason he'd been picked by Reacher for the Special Investigators unit. Reynolds had helped Dave many times, and now, Dave felt like he owed the man.

Reynolds had been a bit of a drinker in the Army, but then again, who hadn't? Dave seemed to vaguely recall some whispers that maybe Reynolds' penchant for the bottle was something more than just a hobby, but he'd never heard one way or the other if it had blossomed into a true addiction.

Dave wondered about the savagery of the crime. Cutting someone into pieces took a certain mindset and skillset. Not to mention an obvious goal: prevent identification. Usually, it was just to prevent detection, to get away with the crime.

But it could also be for additional reasons. Maybe it was a heist gang and they were getting ready for a big score. Or a spree killer who wasn't done with his work just yet.

Random crime was rare and the murder of Joe Reynolds certainly didn't qualify. Dave was betting Joe had gotten too close on one of his cases and his quarry had gotten ahead of him.

It was a bullshit way for a man like Joe Reynolds to leave the world. It pissed off Dave.

He swung his feet from the desk, rolled up to the computer and checked his calendar. He sent off a flurry of emails rearranging meetings and phone calls and then booked himself a direct flight to Boston for the next day.

With that task complete, he shut down his computer, turned out the lights in the office and locked the door behind him. Dave lived in a brownstone not far from Georgetown and it would be his next stop.

A light dinner and then throw a small suitcase together and head to Boston.

He thought of Annette Hazeltine buried in the concrete and then Joe Reynolds cut into pieces and stuffed down a drain.

Well, Philip Hazeltine was going to pay dearly for what he'd done to his wife.

Dave wanted to find the sick bastards who'd killed Joe Reynolds and make them pay, too.

And pay dearly.

Chapter 8

Hornet's nest or not, Steiner and Newsome made short work of New England and were soon crossing the monotonous stretch of Middle America via I-80 and then I-90. They went through Ohio and then followed the signs to Gary, Indiana.

"What a shithole," Steiner said as they hit the outskirts of the city.

"This is worse than Afghanistan," Newsome pointed out.

Along the freeway, a stench of refineries filled the van with a sour smell. Rolling the windows down would have only made it worse. There were smokestacks belching flames and smoke, a thin mist of pollution laded fog everywhere and to the west of the freeway rows of tiny houses no doubt covered with a thin film of grime.

"Bad place to live, good place for a meet," Steiner pointed out.

Newsome steered the van toward a side street and wound his way through a neighborhood, often doubling back and parking on a side street.

"We're clear," he told Steiner after repeated efforts to draw out any kind of tail.

"Let's go," she said.

The meet was to take place in a corner bar with two sets of windows and both a front and back door. The place was called Sully's and Newsome parked the van a block away. He and Steiner split up and approached the establishment from two different directions, checking for spotters and a potential ambush team.

When they met together back near the van, Newsome said, "We're clear. Let's do this."

They entered Sully's and stood several feet apart, ready for any kind of response.

There was none.

A jukebox in the back played a country song full of lap steel guitar, cigarette smoke hung in the air. *Or maybe it's from the refineries*, Newsome thought. On the wall was a faded poster for the movie *Hoosiers*.

Behind the bar a thickset woman with a short-sleeved Cubs t-shirt wiped a beer glass with a dirty towel. Steiner went to the last booth in the corner of the bar and slid in with her back against the wall.

"Two beers," Newsome said to the bartender who nodded in response. She poured a couple of drafts and Newsome slid across a ten-dollar bill.

"Keep the change," he said.

He took the beers to the booth and slid in opposite of Steiner. A mirrored Pabst Blue Ribbon sign hung on the wall and in the reflection, Newsome was able to watch the front door. To the left of Steiner and the right of the mirror was a short hallway with a bathroom on each side. Beyond the bathrooms was the back door that led out to the alley.

Each of them had a vantage point and could provide cover if a quick exit was needed.

Now, all they had to do was wait.

As if she read his mind, Steiner glanced at her phone and then shook her head.

First that damn Joe Reynolds wouldn't leave us alone, and now this, Newsome thought.

He had a bad feeling about the meet, and about their situation. As the team member with the job of tactical planning, he reviewed his actions. Dealing with Reynolds had been a necessity.

Setting up this meeting was also essential.

The only problem was there were certain

things neither he nor Steiner had been able to confirm.

As the minutes turned into a quarter-hour and then a quarter-hour turned into a half hour, Newsome finally made up his mind.

They were going to leave.

Just as he opened his mouth to tell Steiner it was time to bail, the back door opened and gunfire erupted.

Chapter 9

First class wasn't Dave O'Donnell's style, but his long legs definitely required an exit row. So he enjoyed the short flight from DC to Boston and before long he was parking his rental car in front of a cop hangout suggested by Bozel.

Dave spotted the homicide detective at the end of the bar, drinking an amber liquid from a small glass, his eyes on the television screen.

A college basketball game was playing.

"I got twenty bucks riding on this," Bozel said as Dave sat next to him and they shook hands.

Bozel was a thickset man with an enormous chest and a bulging stomach. He had thick arms and his neck and face were red. But his small brown eyes were dark with intelligence and no shortage of street smarts. Dave had seen cops like Bozel before: tough, experienced and instantly aware of all angles. They were usually great at spotting bullshitters, too.

"Thanks for meeting me," Dave said.

Bozel nodded and Dave ordered a beer.

They made small talk for a few minutes about sports and catching up on their shared but limited history before Dave brought up Joe Reynolds.

"So what's not in the report?" Dave asked. A former investigator himself, he knew that homicide reports were written very carefully, in a certain way, and presented as a steady succession of facts. No opinions were allowed as a defense attorney would use them to shred the case.

That meant that a lot of hunches, guesses, and rumors shared by the cops on the scene were absent from the official record.

That's exactly what Dave was after.

"Reynolds had a bit of a niche," Bozel said.

"Oh yeah?"

Bozel stared at the screen and shook his head. "That was a bad shot." He returned to his drink. "Yeah, a specialty."

"And what was it?"

Bozel turned to face Dave. "Rumor was he'd fallen on hard times because of booze and had resorted to working the loonies. And cold cases. Stuff that people had given up on."

"The loonies?"

"Yeah, you know, the lunatics. Crazy people

who think their aunt was abducted by aliens. Or that JFK is bagging groceries at Publix. You know what I mean?"

Dave knew there were a million different kinds of private investigators. From the big corporate firms down to the bottom of the barrel types who weren't much better than criminals themselves.

He just had a hard time reconciling this new image of Joe Reynolds with the one he had in his memory banks.

Bozel must have been able to read the expression on Dave's face because he said, "Hey, it's just a rumor." He glanced back up at the television screen.

Dave thought about conspiracy theorists and how it might have led to someone chopping up Reynolds and stuffing his body parts down a drain.

"Did you find anything in his office?"

"No office. He worked out of his home. Nothing there. Looked to me like a lonely guy with maybe a drinking problem as his only company." Bozel glanced down at the drink in his hand, shrugged, and tossed it back.

"We went through all the court cases he was named in but we didn't find much. But we're still working on it," Bozel said. "Who knows, maybe we overlooked something. But if we didn't, then this is going to be a tough one to crack. One of those where a tip or a new witness will point us in the right direction." He drained the rest of his drink. "I hate those kind, but what are you gonna do?" Bozel got to his feet. "Look, I'll keep you posted. And thanks for the drink."

The big detective left and Dave smiled. He had no idea how long Bozel had been sitting there and how much the tab might be but he didn't mind.

"One last question," he said to Bozel.

The detective paused and glanced back at Dave, an eyebrow raised.

"Any particular crazy case catch your eye?"

Bozel smiled. "You know what, there was one. It had to do with secret government agents." He made his eyes wide with mock fear and then laughed.

"I'll see you around," the detective said.

Dave watched him go and then signaled the bartender for the check.

Secret government agents, he thought.

Chapter 10

Newsome was out of the booth and firing before the back door of the bar was even fully open. A long-barreled weapon, maybe an AK-47, was in the hands of a man with dark skin and a dark shirt. Newsome didn't have time to process anything more.

He simply shot through the door and heard a scream and then the body of another man filled the door. Instead of an automatic rifle, Newsome saw a shotgun.

Newsome dove for the floor as Steiner was up and shooting from the other side of the doorway.

A grenade rolled in from the door and Newsome spun and dove over the bar, with Steiner right behind him, landing on top of his body as the grenade exploded.

The walls shook and bottles of liquor fell from

the shelf, showering the two of them with glass and alcohol. Newsome spotted a half-broken bottle of Jack Daniels. He knocked off the top half and poured a stream into his mouth.

He looked around and saw no sign of the bartender. Was she dead? Or had she been tipped off?

Steiner rolled and came up in a crouch, peering over the top of the bar.

Newsome raced to his left, through a doorway that opened up into a tiny kitchen with a single grease fryer, a dishwasher and an industrial-grade refrigerator. A small window was above the back wall and Newsome climbed onto the stainless steel prep table and peered out the window. A dark car was barreling away from the bar. One of the vehicle's rear doors was open from which a pair of legs dangled.

A hand pulled the legs inside the car and the door was shut.

Newsome hopped down from the table and saw the bartender cowering under the dishwashing station.

He went back into the bar, nodding to Steiner. They both approached the rear entrance and noted the bullet holes.

There was blood but no body.

In the distance, they heard sirens.

Steiner raced through the back door, down the

alley and Newsome followed. They got to their van, fired it up and drove away from the neighborhood. They quickly hopped onto the freeway and didn't stop until an hour later when they were finally in Chicago proper.

They found an abandoned strip mall, parked and got out.

"What did we miss?" Steiner asked.

They'd reloaded their weapons in the van and now looked out at the cold, gray Chicago sky.

"We need to check the van again," Newsome replied. They'd swept it for bugs before the killing of Joe Reynolds, but hadn't done it since.

They each started at opposite ends of the vehicle and within five minutes, Steiner announced, "Here we go."

Newsome walked back to her and she showed him the GPS tracker. No bigger than a ping pong ball.

"It's not even high quality," he pointed out.

He knew he was right. It looked like the kind of thing they'd used ten years ago overseas.

"We're not dealing with the A-Team here, are we?" Steiner asked.

"I think it's safe to say we've got the A-Team, B-Team and every other letter-team looking to take us out," he replied. "We've got to be better and smarter than all of them."

Steiner dropped the tracking device onto the asphalt and crushed it with her boot heel.

"I think it's time we go on the offense," Newsome said.

Steiner nodded. "'Bout time."

Chapter 11

The control room was outside Washington, DC, ironically less than a half mile from the office of Dave O'Donnell.

But this was not a private enterprise.

It was bought and paid for by U.S. tax dollars even though no public mention of the entity appeared in any legislation or budget documents. The money came from an unofficially designated slush fund accessed by less than five people in the combined government/military establishment.

The group had no real name or designation, certainly no acronym so beloved by government officials and budget directors.

Their main "office" was a converted commercial storage warehouse. The front of the space held pallets of paper products. Next to the front door to the unit was a small office with a single desk chair, a table and an old printer covered with dust.

At the rear of the property was a false wall. On the other side was the real enterprise: a series of several offices cloaked with soundproofing material and a control room outfitted with the absolute latest technology: computers, scanners, satellite networks and in a locked room, weapons.

They informally referred to themselves as the *Termination Department*, mainly because the leader of the group had a vague resemblance to the actor Arnold Schwarzenegger back when he made *The Terminator* – a famous action movie about a cyborg sent back in time to kill the unborn leader of the "resistance."

Back then, Schwarzenegger sported a shaggy haircut and black sunglasses, a leather jacket and leather boots. The leader of the Termination Department was also a large man, with broad shoulders and a square face. His fashion sense left much to be desired but despite this, he was widely feared.

His name was Brock and he had a vague background that was comprised of stops in Special Forces, the CIA and some off-the-books freelance work.

Now, he stood with his massive arms folded across his chest and watched the large flat screen connected to their computer network. The oper-

GAME OVER (Jack Reacher's Special Investigators)

ator of the technology was a woman and she had just finished explaining the GPS tracker they'd placed on Newsome and Steiner's vehicle had ceased to operate. In the parking lot of a strip mall in Chicago.

"Great," Brock said. His voice was deep tinged with expected disappointment. Unlike the actor, however, he had no accent. Born and raised in Ohio, he was a purebred American whose commitment to country was extreme.

"What about the satellites?"

Although a small group, the Termination Department had some access to military satellites, however, it was on a shared basis. Meaning, they did not have around-the-clock access.

The woman checked a separate dialogue box on her screen.

"We regain access in thirty minutes."

Brock remained silent.

He stared at the blank map with no target acquired. Thirty minutes before regaining access to satellites was no good to him. The two different groups he wanted to track could be anywhere by then.

The third person in the room was a pale-skinned man with white hair and nearly colorless eyes. His name was Overton. He had silently been observing the news of the events in Gary, Indiana, and now the loss of the tracker in Chicago. He was also watching Brock, a look of expectant curiosity on his face.

It was difficult to assess his age, but his suit was expensive and his demeanor unafraid. Although Brock was a walking monument to intimidation, the albino man seemed oblivious to that fact.

The big man's head swiveled and he locked eyes with Overton.

"Let's move from observation to termination," Brock said.

And then he added, "Send in Tate."

Chapter 12

Dave O'Donnell climbed the stairs to Joe Reynolds' second-floor apartment. He felt a vague sense of sorrow for the dead man. It was less than a half mile from the city center of Boston and the neighborhood had seen better days.

It wasn't that it was a particularly dangerous zip code, just terribly neglected. Dave couldn't help but feel that Reynolds may have felt a kinship with his down-and-out neighbors. He wondered how a man like Reynolds could end up here, with so much intelligence, passion and steadfastness. Dave remembered the rumors of addiction, and if left unchecked, he knew that could wreak havoc on even the most intelligent.

The apartment building was a perfect square of basic construction. No thought had been given to aesthetics. Made of cinderblock painted beige, it featured a central door, and two apartments on the first floor, two on the second floor. The cheapest windows available for builders had been installed and the roof was leaking, half of the gutters were rusted or missing and the landscaping was overgrown. Garbage littered the side street next to the building. Across the street, an old man with a paper bag in his hand watched Dave climb the stairs.

Dave had been one hundred percent certain that Joe Reynolds would not have a separate office for his private investigation cases. If he had indeed been down on his luck with a drinking problem and this was the kind of place he lived, there would have been no way he could afford a separate office with its attendant rent. Bozel had said much the same, but Dave never accepted any information without giving it his careful consideration first. It was too easy for things to be overlooked.

No, this would have been it, he thought.

Now, Dave climbed the stairs and came to the apartment. As always, he had a switchblade in one pocket and a set of ceramic brass knuckles in the other. He also had a slim leather case with lock-picking tools, which he used to easily open the door to Joe Reynolds' apartment. Dave ducked under the single strand of crime scene tape and stepped inside.

GAME OVER (Jack Reacher's Special Investigators)

The place was neat, but smelled like an old man with an additional layer of sour whiskey.

It was a simple layout: a living area off to the right, kitchen to the left. A hallway leading into the back where there was no doubt a bedroom and a bathroom. The carpet was worn and threadbare. An old couch sagged against the wall. A television at least twenty years old sat on an upside-down cardboard box. The middle of the box was slightly caved in and the television was crooked.

One thing Dave had learned in his years as an Army investigator was that preconceptions were just as dangerous as some of the bad folks committing crimes. Which is why he always tried to keep an open mind and be ready for something out of the ordinary.

It explained why he hadn't moved since stepping inside the apartment.

Because standing in the middle of the living room was a woman. In her hand was a gun and it was pointed directly at Dave's chest.

"What took you so long?" asked Frances Neagley.

Chapter 13

The man looked like he had stepped out of a 1970s advertisement for premium cognac. He had gold hair smoothed back and a floral shirt with a big collar underneath a worn leather jacket.

His jeans were slightly flared over brown leather cowboy boots. His sunglasses were vaguely reminiscent of Elvis circa 1972 and behind them, a lean face with a strong jaw and dimpled chin.

His name was Tate and he strolled through Chicago's O'Hare Airport, his eyes taking in the throngs of people waiting at gates, hurried businessmen either on their way to meetings or coming from them. Always easy to tell which. They were neatly buttoned up if they were arriving. If they'd had their meeting and were on their way out of town, their ties were undone and their faces were flushed thanks to three or four martinis at the airport bar. Three if the meeting had gone well, four if it hadn't.

Tate was always amused by them, and felt a smug sense of satisfaction over his choice of profession.

He killed people for money.

There was no need to sugarcoat it. Tate was paid handsomely for his services but what really earned him his premium fee was his discretion. His obsession with never getting caught created a secondary benefit: his employers were protected from scrutiny. A win-win.

Now, Tate picked up his rental car and headed for a specific hotel less than a half mile from O'Hare. There, he retrieved a suitcase from a private locker usually reserved for guests. Tate's current employer had simply paid triple the ordinary fee to rent the locker for twenty-four hours.

Suitcase retrieved, Tate headed out of Chicago toward Indiana.

He considered it Part One of his two-part performance.

The appetizer before the entree.

Tate smiled behind the retro sunglasses as he thought of his favorite quote.

When you love what you do, you never work a day in your life.

Chapter 14

"Neagley," Dave said. He wouldn't consider himself a hugger, but the temptation to embrace his former colleague arose, and then just as quickly dissipated. Frances Neagley had a thing about physical contact. She hated being touched and everyone respected it.

No one asked why, although privately the question had come up. No one had seemed to care too much about the answer as there were only a few realistic options and the desire to delve into those possibilities simply wasn't there. The team of Special Investigators had respected Neagley and her privacy too much.

"You meet with Bozel?" she asked. Dave smiled inwardly. Just like Neagley; all business. And always one step ahead of everyone else.

"Did you smell the beer?" he asked. He took a

good look at her; short, muscular, dark hair and no makeup. Next to Reacher, she had been the toughest and most feared of the Special Investigators.

She cocked her head. "No, the time gap between your flight's arrival and your appearance here was about right for a quick drink with a homicide detective somewhere near the station."

Dave nodded. Of course she knew the details of his flight.

"Didn't get much from him," he said. "Just that Reynolds was down on his luck, drinking too much, working for anyone who would pay his fee."

"Such as?"

"Loonies is what Bozel said. Aliens and secret government agents."

"Money's money," Neagley pointed out.

Dave looked around the place. "How long have you been here?"

"About five minutes before you. So let's take a look."

It was like the old team. Back in the Army, under their leader Jack Reacher, they'd been a well-oiled machine, producing results and working with a lethal precision. *You do not mess with the Special Investigators.* And if you do, Dave thought, you'll get your ass kicked.

Neagley went into Reynolds' bedroom and

Dave went straight to the kitchen table that sat halfway between the kitchen and living room, pushed up against a wall.

The first thing he noticed was under the table. Although relatively neat and organized, Reynolds clearly didn't have a cleaning service as there was a fine layer of dust on the kitchen floor. Except for a series of squares underneath the table.

It looked like a crime scene unit had been in the apartment but that they'd done very little. The handle to the refrigerator was dusted, as well as the door handles but not much else. It technically wasn't a crime scene, but Bozel's team had at least done enough to see if there were any interesting visitors to Reynolds' apartment.

Also, on the surface of the table, Dave found a second rectangle outlined in dust.

Neagley appeared from the bedroom and Dave glanced at her.

"Someone took the boxes underneath here," he said, pointing at the dust outlines. "Probably contained all of his files. And then he had a computer here, probably a laptop."

"Kind of methodical for a bunch of alien-obsessed loonies," she pointed out, suggesting if one of Reynolds' clients had done him in, they'd been fairly professional which usually isn't a trait of the lunatic fringe.

"Yeah, and no sign of forced entry," he

replied. "So not only are they vicious enough to chop him up and shove him down a drain, they know how to pick locks and remove any kind of paper trail, all without getting caught."

"We'll see about that," Neagley said.

She had put on a pair of latex gloves and went to the refrigerator. On the front, a small photo of Reynolds with a couple of Army pals was held in place by a refrigerator magnet from an auto repair shop. The photo was old and Neagley idly wondered if Reynolds looked at those days with nostalgia or disappointment in what he'd become.

Neagley opened the fridge, pulled out two beers, handed one to Dave. They each popped a top and Neagley said, "Cheers."

Neagley put down her beer on the counter and opened all of the cabinets. She saved the one beneath the sink for last. She opened it and pulled out the wastebasket. Inside were three empty bottles of the cheapest whiskey known to man. There was an empty, individual frozen pizza box and crumpled up receipts.

She set the receipts on the kitchen counter and smoothed them out.

Dave brought his beer over and looked over her shoulder. The first receipt was from the grocery store. Beer and a pizza.

The second receipt was from a liquor store.

Two bottles of whiskey for a whopping combined price of ten bucks.

The third was a slip from the library with a code printed in fading ink. 2C.

"No books in the bedroom," Neagley said, looking at the library receipt.

"Nothing in the living room," Dave added. "No books, rented movies, nothing."

Neagley looked around the room and considered their options.

"Time to hit the library," she said. "Finish your beer."

Chapter 15

The intel was always good with this crew. Tate knew of Brock, knew the bare minimum regarding his so-called Termination Department. He'd done a few jobs for them already and there had been no surprises.

Tate's current quarry was on the run; their last stop had been at a cheap motel off the Interstate. From what Tate had been told, the group was a low-level terror cell who'd tried to pull off some kind of heist in a bar in Gary, Indiana, and had gotten their asses handed to them.

They'd probably gotten out of Chicago the fastest way possible and had now stopped to lick their wounds.

Brock's team had sent along a description and the bonus nugget that one or more may have been wounded.

Tate mulled over the information and wondered if Brock had put the group up to it; they had failed, and now he wanted to remove any link between them. It was standard operating procedure with guys like Brock, Tate knew. Happened all the time.

The motel was old, probably built five decades ago and looked like it had seen much better days. The structure was an L-shape with a dozen cars parked in front of their respective rooms. It was called the Lazy Inn and the aluminum siding, originally dark blue, was now speckled with rust and swaths of it were missing. The roof was discolored and the parking lot's asphalt surface was cracked and choked with weeds.

Tate steered his rental car into the far corner of the lot and popped the trunk. He opened the suitcase and saw a set of two pistols, both of them Glock 17s with threaded barrels. Each pistol had a sound suppressor and Tate screwed them into place, then loaded each gun. He put a spare magazine in each pocket although he was fairly confident he wouldn't be needing the extra ammunition.

The car he'd been told to look for was a Ford Taurus – the classic shitty rental car used by the bargain basement car rental companies. They bought cars that had been used and discarded by

GAME OVER (Jack Reacher's Special Investigators)

their bigger competitors and tried to squeeze every last mile they could out of them.

Tate spotted the vehicle in front of Room 17, the third to last room on the right side of the L. He considered the dilemma. Even the dumbest criminals wouldn't park their car directly in front of their room, especially if they had a remote idea someone might be looking for them.

However, he also didn't want to spend all night waiting for some sign of which room was occupied by the Taurus's owner.

Tate got back into his car and pulled up right next to the Taurus. He shut the car off and studied his key fob. First, he hit the Lock button and heard all four doors lock into place. Next, he found the panic button at the very bottom of the fob. He pressed and held it.

The car erupted with the horn honking and his hazards flashing. Tate calmly sat amid the cacophony and studied the doors. After fifteen seconds, he was rewarded with the sight of movement from Room 20, the very last room on the L. The door had been cracked open just the slightest. Tate thumbed the panic button again and his car stopped its auditory assault.

He stepped out of the vehicle and walked purposely toward Room 20. He glanced around the motel and saw no other signs of life. Apparently, a car alarm raised very little interest.

Tate had a Glock in each hand, held down and low in front of him. He stepped up to Room 20 and glanced to his left.

Still no signs of civilians.

He raised the pistols and simultaneously shot two rounds into the door handle mechanism and two rounds into the area of the deadbolt, indicated by the merest shadow between door and jamb. With the sound of the bullets crashing into flimsy particleboard Tate followed with a lowered shoulder and crashed into the door, feeling with satisfaction as it swung open with virtually no resistance.

A dark-skinned man was fumbling with an AK-47 and Tate shot him twice in the face. The man and the gun fell to the floor.

A second man dove for a pistol on a night table next to a bottle of rubbing alcohol. Tate shot him in the back of the head. His blood sprayed onto the already stained wallpaper.

A third man emerged from the bathroom. He wore a light blue T-shirt with blood stains all over the front. He stared into the room with an open mouth, seemingly unable to comprehend what he was seeing.

Not exactly a man of action, Tate thought, as he put one bullet into the mouth, saw the teeth spray like confetti. The second round tore open the man's forehead and blew out the back of his skull.

GAME OVER (Jack Reacher's Special Investigators)

Tate stepped over the dead man into the bathroom and saw a fourth man in the tub. His eyes were wide. He was already dead.

Tate shot him anyway.

Back in the room, the scent of blood and body fluids filled the air. An open suitcase held clothes, disposable cell phones and a jumbo bag of potato chips. Still wearing leather gloves, Tate tore open the bag of potato chips and ate a few. As he crunched, he considered his next move. Secretly, he'd been hoping these idiots had been carrying cash, but obviously that wasn't the case.

He looked more closely at the face of the first man he'd shot. Middle Eastern for sure. Same with the other three. All with bushy beards. Prayer mats were neatly stacked in the corner of the room.

Killing a group of amateur terrorists brought no special joy to Tate.

What did bring him joy were the free chips.

He carried the bag outside with him, got into his rental car and drove away, heading west.

Intermission was over.

Part Two of his performance had now begun.

Chapter 16

According to the little map of the library, the quiet section was on the third floor while restricted books were on the second along with research cubicles and a computer lab. The restrooms were on the first floor by the magazine and fiction shelves, along with the locker bay.

Dave and Neagley walked directly to the lockers where a sign informed them the small community college library had lockers, but they were only for currently enrolled students.

"Do you think he was taking classes here?" Dave asked.

"Doubt it," Neagley said. "But he couldn't afford to rent a storage box somewhere so he probably figured out a way to get one. Maybe he found a student ID somewhere, or he talked one into lending him their library card for a minute."

GAME OVER (Jack Reacher's Special Investigators)

"Resourceful."

Neagley headed straight for locker 2C. The keys were the old-fashioned kind with a big orange plastic knob for a handle.

She stepped aside and let Dave, whose lock-picking finesse was unmatched among the Special Investigators, get the locker open. It took him less than five seconds.

He swung the door open and inside was a single file folder, slim, held shut with a single small paper clip.

"There we go," Dave said.

Together, they carried it over to a table next to a rack of magazines all beginning with the letter M; *Mac Life*, *Mademoiselle*, *Menopause Matters*, which Dave figured probably didn't get much use on a college campus.

Neagley flipped open the file and saw a sheet of paper with the name Gideon. A series of numbers were listed below it.

Dave didn't recognize anything about the name or the numbers.

"These numbers mean nothing to me," Neagley said. "Gideon was a figure in the Bible – a warrior, I believe."

She turned that sheet of paper over and saw the logo of the Department of Defense. It was a series of photographs, most likely shot by a satellite, of what clearly represented the aftermath of a battle.

There were no written descriptions or captions accompanying the images.

Finally, the last sheet of paper was a photo of a man and a woman.

The man stared into the camera, his face blank. He had short hair, a thick jaw and small eyes.

The woman was brunette, with black hair tied back into a ponytail and a small nose. Her lips were drawn and her wide eyes seemed angry and capable of cruelty.

"Ring a bell?" Neagley asked.

"No."

She shut the file and tucked it under her arm.

"Let's go to my hotel. I need my computer." She glanced at Dave. "Where are you staying?"

"Nowhere as of yet."

"I'll get you a room next to mine."

They left the library and didn't notice the dark blue Chevy sedan parked halfway down the block.

Inside were two men. One had his hands on the wheel.

The other had a camera and was using burst mode to take multiple pictures at once.

The sound of the shutter clicking filled the silence in the car.

Chapter 17

The drive from Chicago to Sioux Falls, South Dakota, took Newsome and Steiner less than eight hours. Newsome drove. Steiner looked out the window, occasionally giving her opinion on the status of their mission.

"Got to plug the leak," she repeated. Steiner had already said the phrase a half dozen times and Newsome had stopped responding. Besides, she knew he was in agreement.

She thought back to the scene at the bar in Gary. Bush league, she thought. Multiple attackers coming in through the same door? They should have used separate angles. Or created a diversion at the front door.

Her critique wasn't just limited to the attackers, though. Because if they were indeed relatively unskilled, maybe even amateurish, how come she and Newsome hadn't killed or captured one of them?

To get one alive would have been an ideal scenario.

They could have thrown him in the van and tortured him to find the leak. It wouldn't have taken long. Torture was one of her specialties. She had perfected it in the Middle East, come to enjoy it on a sexual level. Some of the best sex she'd ever had was immediately after she'd tortured someone and gotten the information she wanted. And then killed them.

Now, as she thought about how much fun it would have been to capture and mutilate one of their attackers from the bar in Gary, she felt herself getting aroused. Steiner pushed the sensation back down and out of her mind.

Not now, she thought.

Newsome drove their new vehicle – they'd ditched the van in Wisconsin and used cash to buy a four-wheel drive pickup truck – and exited I-90 and headed south into Sioux Falls proper.

When they crossed the Big Sioux River, Newsome turned into the drive of a corporate business park with multiple high-rises and a vast parking lot.

There was a list of businesses at the entrance on a long sign.

Third from the bottom was a name that caught Steiner's eye.

Gideon, Inc.

Chapter 18

Neagley's hotel was one of the high-end chains that tended to attract business executives who don't want to stray too far from the airport. She had a big room with a sitting area and a kitchenette.

Dave put coffee on while Neagley retrieved her laptop.

She used the scanner on her phone to make digital copies of the papers from the file.

Neagley sent the first set of copies to Edgar Chavez, a computer genius and former member of the Special Investigators. He had a consulting business in Venice, Florida, and did quite well for himself providing top-level cyber security to clients all over the world.

The second set went to Karla Dixon, with a special request from Neagley to study the odd set of numbers beneath the name Gideon. Dixon had been a member of the original Special Investigators under Reacher and her specialty had been financial crimes. She had been Reacher's equal, or some might say, better, when it came to numbers.

Dave stood behind her sipping his coffee and then he handed her a cup. It was black. Another habit they'd acquired from Jack Reacher.

Neagley studied the numbers and thought about how Reacher and Dixon used to go back and forth over numbers and mathematical equations. It sometimes amused her and sometimes annoyed her.

"She'll have a half dozen theories within the hour," Dave pointed out.

It was true. Dixon was a machine with numbers, or more accurately, a calculator.

"Chavez should have a good facial recognition system," Neagley said. "Linked to every database in the world, practically."

"Doesn't your firm have one?"

Neagley was a founding partner of an international security powerhouse back in Chicago. She was a very wealthy woman.

"Yeah, but I would have to jump through a hoop or two. Chavez will be faster. And it will be easier for him to bend a few rules."

"Something's bugging me about those photos," Dave said.

"Not the best quality. Maybe Chavez can improve them."

"It's not that. There's something about the way they're posed."

"You mean like driver's license photographs?"

Dave shook his head. He wasn't sure what it was.

The looks on their faces? Or the positioning of their bodies?

It was something about their expressions. Like they were angry about something.

Suddenly, he snapped his fingers.

"That's it," he said.

Neagley looked at him.

"Do you see the way they're looking? Those aren't government ID photos. Or driver's license pictures."

"Then what are they?"

Dave smiled.

"Mug shots," he said.

Chapter 19

Karla Dixon sat in the coffee shop on her lunch break and studied the screen of her phone. It was a message from Frances Neagley.

It was classic Neagley: an economy of words: *Any insight?*

Followed by a series of numbers.

Dixon smiled. That's what she loved about Neagley: all business. Dixon pictured her – solid, muscular, short dark hair. Dixon caught her own reflection in the glass window of the coffee shop; in a business suit with her hair back and the clean lines of her face, she looked about as opposite as possible from Neagley.

She shook off the thought and studied the numbers. It was like all of the noise and commotion around her faded away as the digits rolled across her consciousness.

They were all the same: eight numerals. The first five separated from the last three by a hyphen.

The first one was 40087-083.

All of the usual suspects were readily dismissed: driver's license, social security, tax ID, addresses, phone numbers. Dixon worked for a financial services company as their chief forensic investigator. She made a top salary for her expertise.

Because of her vast experience in the banking industry, she immediately dismissed most types of account numbers. Even international routing IDs, Swiss accounts, Bahamian hideouts.

Of course, she also knew they could be totally mundane. Product codes. A company's internal filing system.

Her coffee forgotten and the internal clock on her lunch hour turned off, Dixon hunched forward. She couldn't help but think back to Reacher and their shared love of numbers. Later, on a case in Los Angeles, they'd shared quite a bit more.

Dixon waved the memories away and focused.

Obviously, the hyphen was the key. Two different identifiers. The first set of numbers identified one thing. The second set represented additional information. Or perhaps it was the other way around. The first set was the primary, the second set was the qualifier.

It was possible.

The first set would most likely be the customized number meant to be more specific. The second set would be a larger classification. It was the way the human mind worked.

Product codes for instance. A chair comes in twelve different colors. The product code lists the main product (chair) followed by its variation: the color.

These weren't product codes, however. Frances Neagley ran a high-powered security firm in the second–largest city in the country. She wouldn't be sending IDs for patio furniture to her former colleague.

Maybe if they were military weapons, but Dixon knew all too well the way the government liked to label their hardware and those tended to be much longer and usually have multiple strings of letters. No one loved acronyms more than the U.S. government.

She cocked her head.

That was interesting.

The military.

That was obviously what linked Dixon and Neagley. Their time together chasing down bad guys as military investigators. Catching wrongdoers and locking them up–

And then it hit Dixon like the burst of a beautiful, forgotten memory.

She smiled and picked up her phone.

Chapter 20

"Military prisoners," Dixon said to Neagley, who was on the other end of the line. Neagley had her cell phone to her ear and glanced at Dave who had a smirk on his face.

"Yeah, Dave figured it out, too," Neagley said. "The photos were mug shots and then we kind of went from there."

Dave mouthed the words "Thank you" to Neagley.

"Thanks," she added to Dixon. "Anyway."

Neagley disconnected the call, shrugged her shoulders and studied the numbers.

"Eight military prisoners," Neagley said. "So why was Reynolds investigating?"

"We need to find out who they were," Dave replied.

"I sent the update to Chavez who's got a line

into the Pentagon's personnel files – don't ask me how."

"Good."

"But even if we get the names, we need to think one step ahead. What do they mean? Why are they important? How are they linked to Reynolds?"

"Maybe one of them was wrongly convicted," Dave said. "Happens all the time. You see news stories where guys are being freed with new DNA testing. Bozel said Reynolds was working cold cases. Maybe one of the prisoners contacted Reynolds, asked him to look into the case, claiming that he's innocent."

"Everyone in prison claims they're innocent," Neagley said. "Some other guy did it."

Dave didn't argue with her.

"Or maybe he was taking on a crime one of them committed before they got locked up," Neagley said. "You know how serial killers are always being linked to new victims even after they've been in prison for twenty years."

"Possible," Dave admitted.

Neagley's email pinged and she opened up the message.

"Chavez," she said.

"What'd he find?"

Neagley was reading the email. It didn't take her long.

"Dead."

"One of them is dead? Which one?"

"No," Neagley answered. "Not which one."

Dave looked at her, disbelief in his eyes.

"They're dead. All of them."

Chapter 21

The doors of the main entrance to the office building opened and a man emerged. He was big and broad across the shoulders, but with a belly hanging over his pants and the tired, beleaguered demeanor of a desk jockey who's put in a long day.

"There he is," Steiner said.

"Christ, he looks like hell," Newsome pointed out.

The man from the building crossed the parking lot and climbed into a small, late-model sedan. He backed out of his parking space and exited the lot at the opposite end from Newsome and Steiner.

They'd planned it that way.

Newsome put their truck into gear and followed.

Their target drove quickly and aggressively, often forgoing the use of turn signals. He stopped at a convenience store, went inside and came back out with a twelve-pack of beer.

"That explains a few things," Steiner commented.

The man got back into his car and drove to a condominium complex. They were two-story townhomes with peeling paint and missing shutters. He parked in a spot with the number 302 above the carport's roof and went into 302.

"Lazy and sloppy," Newsome said. "Ray used to be halfway decent."

"Civilian life will do that to you."

"Let's let him have a few beers and then we'll go in," Newsome said.

Thirty minutes later, Steiner retrieved a bag from the trunk along with a tire iron and felt the first surges of adrenaline, tinged with sexual arousal, course through her veins.

Newsome led the way to 302 and slid the flat end of the tire iron between the lock and the doorjamb. He pivoted, a short violent twist against the iron and heard with satisfaction as the lock broke free from the jamb.

Steiner rushed past him into the room with her gun drawn.

"Hey Ray," she said.

The man they'd followed was in a leather

chair, his feet up on an ottoman, watching ESPN. There were three empty beer cans on a side table next to him and a fourth beer in his hand.

"You," he said. He had a head of thin hair going gray, a red nose with broken capillaries and tufts of gray chest hair sticking out the top of a stained T-shirt.

Newsome closed the door and secured the broken jamb with a zip tie fastened around the internal deadbolt.

Steiner went behind the man in the chair as Newsome leveled his pistol at him.

"Hold still, Ray," Newsome said. "We're not here to hurt you."

"Yeah right."

"We just want some information."

Steiner pushed the man to his feet and made sure he had no weapons.

"Christ, what happened to you, Ray?" she asked him.

"Life happened, that's what." His voice was a deep baritone and he seemed resigned to his fate. Newsome wondered if Ray was even bothering to consider his options. He was now too big and too slow for any kind of quick action.

Newsome glanced at the television screen. He found the remote and turned the volume up.

"Who leaked our mission, Ray?"

"Come on, man, I don't know. I'm a peon at

Gideon now – do you really think they tell me anything?"

"Yeah, we do," Steiner said.

"I'm not going to ask again, Ray."

"And I'm not going to tell you a lie just to try to make you happy," Ray said. "I don't know anything. That's the truth. I'm low man on the totem pole."

"I can't tell you how excited that makes me feel," Steiner said. She raised a handheld Taser to Ray's neck and pulled the trigger.

The fat man fell to the ground, his body pulsating with spasms.

Newsome pulled a chair over and sat down.

"I know you get off doing this, but let's not dawdle," he said.

Steiner's face was flushed as she withdrew a set of knives, garden shears and a blowtorch.

Chapter 22

"Classified."

Dave and Neagley looked at the computer screen. It was an image sent by Chavez of the roadblock he'd hit finding out more about the military prisoners who were all deceased.

I don't mess with the Pentagon, Chavez had written.

"Can't blame him," Dave pointed out.

"There's got to be a way," Neagley said. She studied the scant information from Chavez.

There was no date assigned to the deaths. No way to find out how, where or why they died.

Well, not exactly.

"Hold on," Neagley said. "The numbers."

"Yeah, they're prisoner numbers."

"No, the first number is the prisoner's ID. But what's the second number?"

Neagley speed dialed Dixon who picked up on the first ring.

"You said you figured out the numbers," Neagley said.

"But not before Dave did," Dixon replied. "Do me a favor – give him an elbow in the ribs from me."

"Of course," Neagley said. "In the meantime, what exactly did you figure out, though?"

"What do you mean?"

"What do the numbers actually represent?"

There was a pause. "The first set of numbers is the actual prison number," Dixon answered. "The five digits represent their actual ID. The second set of numbers, the three digits, is a designation for the location of their crime. As in, where it was committed."

"They're all the same," Neagley said. "083. Did you find out where that is?"

"Sure did," Dixon replied. "It was buried in the Department of Defense's prisoner database."

"And where is 083?"

Dixon paused.

"Northern Afghanistan," she said. "The area of Mazar-i-Sharif to be exact."

Chapter 23

All was quiet in the Termination Department command center. Brock was sitting in the back of the room and hadn't said a word in over an hour. It was assumed he was asleep but on the rare occasion when someone was foolish enough to ask him a question, he responded promptly.

At the same time, the rumor was that he never slept. A true night owl. Dozed occasionally during the day, and hunted in the cover of darkness.

His opposite and the wild card in the department was the albino Overton. Not only was he awake, but he was always wired, as if he'd had a triple espresso a half hour ago. His pale eyes darted everywhere at once and when he spoke, the person he was addressing fought the urge to look over their shoulder to see if he was talking to someone else.

GAME OVER (Jack Reacher's Special Investigators)

Most folks who passed through the Termination Department were scared of both Brock and Overton, but for different reasons. Brock was just a scary, intimidating presence. Overton made people nervous.

Now, he received a message on his secure laptop and closed his eyes. Pink half-moons represented his eyelids and when they finally snapped back open, he got to his feet and approached Brock.

"Bad news," he said.

Brock, who had his size 15 boots up on the edge of a desk, swung them down and sat up straighter. Behind his dark glasses, his eyebrows raised.

"A freelancer tried to hack his way into the Gideon files. He was rebuffed, but probably learned the bare minimum."

"Who is this freelancer?"

"We've been crunching the data for two hours and narrowed it down to southwest Florida. What's interesting is we were able to place a cyber tag on the data and it was promptly sent, via a basic rerouting application which with great effort we managed to untangle, to a hotel room outside Boston registered to a business called Pinnacle Security."

"Get to the point, Overton."

"The founder of that company is one

Frances Neagley, a former military investigator. She was part of a team headed by one Jack Reacher. Another member of the team is Edgar Chavez, who runs a cyber security company based out of southwest Florida in a small town called Venice."

"So Neagley and Chavez are working together on this thing?"

"It would appear so."

"Boston, huh?" Brock asked. The weary tone in his voice again.

"Indeed. Brought there no doubt by our friends butchering Joe Reynolds," Overton said with visible disgust.

"So they killed Reynolds because he was getting too close and now, instead of having one former military investigator trying to track them down, they have a whole team of them?" Brock gazed at the ceiling and his huge hands flexed, as if he were imagining choking the life out of someone.

"Sounds about right."

"I just love how this day is unfolding," Brock said, his fatigued voice now laced with sarcasm.

"This could be even worse than Reynolds," Overton offered.

Brock heaved himself to his feet and looked around the room. Apparently, he didn't like what he saw because he shook his massive head.

"As long as they still have it, not all is lost," he said.

"There is still time," Overton agreed.

"Where the hell is Tate?" Brock asked.

"He took out our friends in Indiana, and now he's on his way to rendezvous with our favorite pair in South Dakota. The satellites were able to pick up their vehicle switch and the license plate was spotted in Sioux Falls."

Brock's smile was more of a grimace.

"Sioux Falls, huh?" He sighed. "Well, I'll give them this: they are not afraid to act and act quickly. I have a feeling they know someone who has the information they're looking for."

"Do you think this person will give it to them?"

Brock laughed out loud. "That bitch is crazy. She loves to torture people. Believe me, if they get their hands on someone with the information they want, it'll come out, one way or the other."

Overton instantly understood what Brock meant.

"What about the investigator in Boston?" he asked.

"I'm in the mood for a little road trip," Brock said, cracking his knuckles. "Besides, I'm tired of delegating."

He held up his huge, meaty paws.

"Time to take matters into my own hands. "

Chapter 24

Neagley drove. Dave stretched out his long legs as far as they would go.

"Are you going to tell me where we're going?" he asked.

"Back to the beginning. Back to Joe Reynolds."

"He is the link," Dave said. "But you're still not telling me where we're going and why."

"Back to his apartment. There's something we missed. It's pissing me off," she said.

"I think you want to help yourself to his beer again," Dave said. "You always were frugal to a fault."

Neagley said nothing and instead, she pressed the accelerator to the floor.

Dave laughed.

They went to the apartment and this time the

crime scene tape was gone. Dave picked the lock again and they went inside. Nothing had changed. The same dust, faded carpet and sagging furniture.

This time, though, Dave went into the bedroom and Neagley took the living area.

He went over everything: the bed, under the mattress, behind the drawers in the dresser. Anywhere and everywhere as the saying went.

By the time he was done, his nose was twitching from dust. He methodically put everything back into place.

Dave made his way into the kitchen.

Neagley was standing in front of the refrigerator.

Dave was about to make another joke about free beer but instead, he followed her gaze.

A photo on the front of the fridge showed Reynolds with two friends in the Army. Dave guessed the photo had been taken some time ago.

He stood behind Neagley and since he was tall and she was short, her head didn't obstruct his vision.

"This is what we missed," she said. She reached up and with one finger, tapped the photo on the front of the fridge.

Dave studied the photo. Reynolds was in the middle and on his left was a man. He was bigger than Reynolds, with a classic warrior face: strong jaw, piercing eyes and a clear attitude. An alpha male. Reynolds had his arm around his shoulders. His other arm was around the person on his right.

She was a short woman, solid, with a blank expression. Dark hair, dark eyes and thin lips. Maybe, just barely, the corner of her mouth was struggling to curve upward and make just the tiniest of smiles.

"They're MPs," Dave said, noticing the uniform and their insignia.

"Yeah. All three," Neagley replied.

Dave leaned forward and read the names on the left breast pocket of their uniforms.

"Newsome and Steiner," he said.

Chapter 25

Dave fished out the papers they'd originally gotten from the file Reynolds had hidden in the library. He held up the photo he was sure were mug shots.

He compared them to the people in the photo on the fridge.

"Nope," he said.

Neagley had her phone in her hand. She was typing out a furious message.

"Chavez can't break into the Pentagon," she said. "But he can certainly get into the files of the CID in Afghanistan."

Dave knew she was right. The Criminal Investigation Command oversaw the Military Police Corp. If Reynolds served with the man and the woman in the Army, Chavez ought to be able to find out who they were and what happened to them.

But something troubled Dave. "How do you know they're involved?"

Neagley walked into the living room and did a slow turn.

"Think about it. Reynolds is looking into cold cases. Secret government agents, right?" she reasoned. "He's got a photo of two people, a man and a woman, in a secret file he hides in the library."

Dave nodded.

Neagley pointed out the walls of the living room.

"Take a look around," she said. "What do you see?"

He knew what she was getting at. "Blank walls," he answered.

"Exactly."

She stepped back into the kitchen and pointed at the fridge.

"Why do people post things on the front door of their refrigerator?" she asked.

"Because it's something they'll look at every day. An inspirational quote. A reminder to stick to their diet."

"Right. And so Reynolds wanted to see this picture every day for a reason. When Bozel said Reynolds was working for loonies, he was wrong. Joe Reynolds wasn't working for someone else. He was working for *himself*."

Dave hadn't moved from his spot. He stared at the photo. "Something happened to this Newsome and Steiner," he said. "It's gotta be a cold case. That's what he was after. And if it was something he wanted to remind himself every day, it wasn't a good thing."

Neagley's phone buzzed and she glanced down.

"Chavez," she said.

She buzzed through the email and then glanced up at Dave.

"They went AWOL," she said.

"Newsome and Steiner?"

"Yeah."

"When?"

She read the message on her phone.

"Right after an attack in Afghanistan that killed a whole bunch of people."

She finished reading and looked up at Dave.

"Including a group of military prisoners."

Chapter 26

Steiner's orgasm occurred when she was halfway through cutting off Ray's head. It went from her core and blossomed throughout every inch of her body, bringing her to a gasping, shuddering climax.

Yet, during it all, the saw blade never stopped moving.

Newsome watched with a mixture of awe and disbelief.

When it was all over, he helped her load the body parts into a black garbage bag and they carried it out together to the apartment complex's dumpster.

Back in the apartment, they covered the blood stains with a throw rug. They weren't concerned with being caught, they just wanted to delay any problems.

The torture had been a success, which came as no surprise to Newsome. Steiner had no equal in that regard.

Ray had coughed up a name.

Brock Dobler.

A giant spook of a man who knew all too well what they were trying to do. Newsome was pretty sure he'd met the man at some point in the service, and he'd definitely heard of him. He and Steiner knew someone was after what they had and wanted to get it before they sold it to the highest bidder. The fact that it was a man like Dobler didn't surprise Newsome but it didn't make him feel any better, either.

"We've got one last chance," Newsome said, always the tactician. "We've got to make the sale happen in the next twenty-four hours or it's over."

Steiner was washing the blood off her hands and arms.

"That's the worst-case scenario," she said. "We've been carrying this shit around for all this time? Hiding out, pretending, trying to make a sale and now we're going to give up?"

"Think about it," Newsome said. "Brock is on to us. That means the CIA, or some other shadow branch of the military. What did he call his team?"

"The Termination Department."

"Yeah, I remember now. He does look like Schwarzenegger."

"He's bad news."

"Not just Brock. It's his team's resources. Because they're official – he can use satellites, the NSA and wiretapping, all kinds of stuff. That's why I'm giving us twenty-four hours."

Steiner checked her phone. "Still no word from Hasanzai."

"That's because he's dead!" Newsome shouted at her. He looked at her in disbelief, then regained his composure. "Don't you realize – with Brock on our tail he's got every weapon at his disposal. After that disaster in Indiana, he certainly found out about it and sent someone to take out Hasanzai. Who knows, Hasanzai might have been working for Brock and his team. We sell it to them, and then Brock takes them out. A lot easier than messing with us and possibly exposing them."

"Then who are we going to sell to?"

Newsome looked down at the dead man on the floor.

"Gideon," he said.

Chapter 27

Edgar Chavez tore his eyes away from the turquoise blue waters of the Gulf of Mexico. His office in Venice, Florida, had a bank of windows that provided loads of natural light and a stunning view of the ocean.

But at the moment, he wasn't interested in the calming effect of the incredible view.

He was worried about Neagley and O'Donnell.

His system was one of the best in the world, but when he'd sent in some virtual scouts to the Pentagon's highly secure network, it hadn't gone unnoticed. On the way back from their errand, his scouts had been tagged and carried with them a set of digital trackers.

In other words, the alarm bells had started ringing.

Chavez had easily disabled the trackers and erased their existence along with his history, but he feared the damage had been done.

He was no stranger to hiding his IP, but the responding digital trackers had come at him with surprising speed and power. Military-grade of the highest order.

Someone knew what he was looking for.

Someone at the Pentagon.

That was the bad news.

The good news was that he had been able to spend just enough time in both the Pentagon's military prisoner database to run a comparison with the numbers Neagley had sent him, along with the photos.

The results had stunned him.

He forwarded his information to Neagley with a warning expressed with four words:

Be careful. They noticed.

Chapter 28

This time, Dave was behind the wheel.

Neagley had the paperwork on her lap and her laptop balanced on one knee. She'd used her phone's hotspot to connect to the web and download Chavez's message.

"Those bastards," she said.

"What?"

Neagley looked at the images on the computer screen and then at the mug shots in the file.

She pointed to the mug shots from the front door of Reynolds' fridge. "These two were prisoners. The guy's name is Harris. The woman's Jennings. They were private contractors working for a company called Gideon and they were accused of stealing a good amount of plutonium from a dirty Pakistani soldier. He'd killed a group of Taliban soldiers and discovered the stuff."

"But they're dead now, right? Jennings and Harris. Killed in the attack, right?"

Neagley smiled.

"Joe Reynolds had it figured out."

"Had what figured out?"

"Don't you see? Newsome and Steiner were MPs, guarding the prisoners. All the prisoners died. Why would Newsome and Steiner go AWOL?"

Dave saw the truth. "Ah," he said.

"Yeah, they didn't go AWOL. They died. But Harris and Jennings survived and stole their identities. Look how similar they are?"

Dave glanced down and saw that Neagley was right. Pretty close in terms of physical appearance.

"These two dirtbags put on the MP uniforms, got rescued, probably sent to the hospital and then quietly melted away."

"With the plutonium," Dave said.

"Exactly," Neagley said. "Reynolds wasn't just trying to solve the disappearance of his two pals, he was trying to stop the sale of a nuclear bomb."

"Shit," Dave said. "Secret government agents. Reynolds wasn't crazy. He was right. Someone over in Spookland already knows about Harris and Jennings. Knows about the plutonium."

"Chavez said they know about us, too."

"Great," Dave said.

The sound of his words was still in the air when the car's windows exploded.

Chapter 29

Tate had watched the pair calling themselves Newsome and Steiner dump a trash bag full of something heavy into the apartment building's dumpster.

He was under no illusions: the bag contained what was left of Ray Sullivan, former employee of Gideon, Inc.

He also knew Newsome and Steiner weren't their real names. It was Harris and Jennings, two private security contractors gone rogue.

He'd watched them follow the hapless man from the headquarters of Gideon, Inc. to his apartment and then Tate had decided to wait, and do a bit of handiwork.

The plutonium had been easy to find – where else can you keep twenty pounds of radioactive material? It had been in the pair's vehicle – the bed of the pickup truck had a hidden compartment and while they'd been inside hacking up Mr. Sullivan, he'd relocated the plutonium into his own possession and left the treacherous couple a little surprise.

Now, he watched them leave the apartment and climb into the truck.

Tate smiled, heard the ignition catch and then the truck went up in one glorious flame.

"Ooh, I love fireworks," Tate said. He put his car into gear and drove away.

Chapter 30

Dave rolled out of the passenger seat and dropped onto the pavement. A shard of glass had sliced open the skin on his forehead above his right eye and blood was running into his eyeball.

He closed it and pulled the gun from his shoulder holster. It was a 9mm and he immediately knew he was outgunned.

Dave glanced over the hood of the car and saw a giant of a man standing in the middle of street looking like John Wayne at high noon. Dave fired instantly, a string of shots grouped tightly and he saw the man barely stagger back.

Bullets tore into the car in reply and Dave ducked back, looked inside the car.

Neagley was gone.

Where was she?

Dave used the sleeve of his shirt to wipe the

blood from his eye and he crabbed his way to the other end of the car. Once there, he dared a quick glance over the trunk.

Neagley was standing over the man with the rifle who was now on his back.

How did she get over there? Dave wondered.

He got to his feet and watched as the big man on the ground tried to pull a pistol from his waistband.

Neagley shot him in the head.

Dave decided to reclassify his ranking of the Special Investigators.

Neagley was even scarier than Reacher.

Chapter 31

Tate met the man at the Sioux Falls airport. They'd used disposable cell phones to communicate their location and since the airport was a regional enterprise, it had been fairly simple to find one another.

Tate's employer had flown in just to take delivery of the product "and to pay the assassin a handsome bonus. It had worked out better than anyone could have imagined. Tate allowed himself the brief fantasy of what he was going to do with his paycheck. Right now, he was leaning toward taking a year off, vacation in an island off the coast of Thailand where he could live like a king with his very own harem. And if he got tired of them, he'd just simply swap them out for some fresh stock.

They walked out to long-term parking and the man studied Tate.

"You really outdid yourself this time," Overton said.

Tate studied the strange-looking man. An albino. White hair. Pasty face. Translucent eyes. It had come as a surprise. Tate had worked with Brock for the most part, and had been expecting the big man. There'd been a rumor Brock had some kind of mysterious partner but Tate had never met him.

Until now.

"Where's Brock?" Tate asked.

"He's on assignment."

"What's your name again?" Tate asked. He was curious why the man was here and not Brock.

"Overton."

"Is that your first or last name?"

"Last."

"What's your first?"

Overton smiled and stuck a gun into Tate's ribs.

"Gideon," he said and pulled the trigger.

Chapter 32

They had matching hospital beds.

It had taken twenty stitches to sew up Dave's wound.

Neagley had been shot in the calf muscle. While not remotely fatal, it had been painful and the doctors had pulled out pieces of metal and sewn up the wound. There was always danger of infection, so she was given antibiotics and told to rest.

Neagley knew that wasn't going to happen.

She and Dave looked at each other.

"You do not mess with the special investigators," Neagley said.

"Yeah, who was that guy?"

Neagley glanced up at the television screen in the corner of the room.

"I have a feeling we'll find out soon enough."

Chapter 33

Overton, also known as Gideon, studied the plutonium in the trunk of Tate's rental car. He was surprised to see a small digital readout on the far right corner of the container. It had a number and it was active.

He glanced down at Tate. He was surprised at how easy it had been to dispatch the hired killer. He was rumored to be one of the best but Overton had caught him by surprise, lulling him into dull greed over the mention of a huge bonus.

Tate's eyes were wide in death and Overton was nervously overjoyed. He smiled.

But then Tate blinked.

And smiled back at Overton.

He held up his hand.

In his palm was a cell phone and his thumb was on a green button.

"No," Overton whispered.

Tate pressed the little green button and the world instantly turned bright red.

Epilogue

Dave and Neagley were seated next to each other in Boston's private luxury club at the airport. Dave had a beer, Neagley a glass of water.

They were watching the news report of a car bomb exploding outside the Sioux Falls airport.

The news reporter stated that two people had died and the bomb had been a small one.

"How the hell could that be?" Dave asked. "Twenty pounds of plutonium."

"It wasn't plutonium," Neagley said. "I'm not surprised."

"All of this over a con job," Dave said. "That Pakistani guy convinced someone he had real plutonium. He probably had a tiny sample that was the real deal, the rest of it was bullshit," Dave said.

"Yeah," she responded. Neagley looked at her phone, an odd expression on her face.

Dave studied her. There was something off. She seemed…happy.

"Hey," Neagley said. "Wanna see a picture of my dog?"

"Sure," Dave said, frowning.

Neagley knew people were always surprised when she offered to share something personal.

She tilted the phone and showed Dave the picture she'd been looking at.

"Cute hound," he said. "What's his name?"

Neagley smirked.

"Reacher," she said.

Dave laughed and sprayed beer onto the counter.

"Let me guess, he doesn't follow orders," Dave said.

"Oh no, his training is going well," Neagley said. "Like most men, he just needed a strong woman."

BUY THE NEXT BOOK IN
THE SERIES!

LIGHTS OUT: BOOK 3 IN JACK
REACHER'S SPECIAL INVESTIGATORS

CLICK HERE TO BUY NOW

A USA TODAY
BESTSELLING BOOK

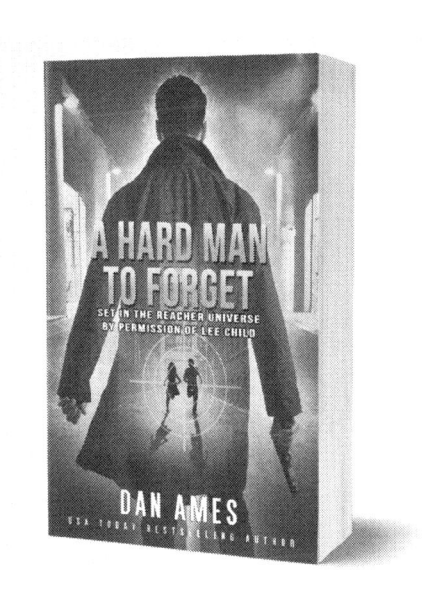

Book One in The JACK REACHER Cases

CLICK HERE TO BUY NOW

A Fast-Paced Action-Packed Thriller Series

CLICK HERE TO BUY

An Award-Winning
Bestselling Mystery Series

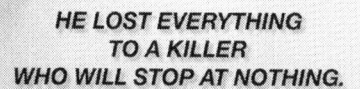

Buy DEAD WOOD, the first John Rockne Mystery.

CLICK HERE TO BUY

"Fast-paced, engaging, original."
-*NYTimes bestselling author Thomas Perry*

About the Author

Dan Ames is a USA TODAY Bestselling Author, Amazon Kindle #1 bestseller, GoodReads Readers Choice finalist and winner of the Independent Book Award for Crime Fiction.

www.authordanames.com
dan@authordanames.com

Also by Dan Ames

THE JACK REACHER CASES

The JACK REACHER Cases #1 (A Hard Man To Forget)

The JACK REACHER Cases #2 (The Right Man For Revenge)

The JACK REACHER Cases #3 (A Man Made For Killing)

The JACK REACHER Cases #4 (The Last Man To Murder)

The JACK REACHER Cases #5 (The Man With No Mercy)

The JACK REACHER Cases #6 (A Man Out For Blood)

The JACK REACHER Cases #7 (A Man Beyond The Law)

The JACK REACHER Cases #8 (The Man Who Walks Away)

The JACK REACHER Cases (The Man Who Strikes Fear)

The JACK REACHER Cases (The Man Who Stands Tall)

The JACK REACHER Cases (The Man Who Works Alone)

The Jack Reacher Cases (A Man Built For Justice)

The JACK REACHER Cases #13 (A Man Born for Battle)

The JACK REACHER Cases #14 (The Perfect Man for Payback)

The JACK REACHER Cases #15 (The Man Whose Aim Is True)

The JACK REACHER Cases #16 (The Man Who Dies Here)

The JACK REACHER Cases #17 (The Man With Nothing To Lose)

The JACK REACHER Cases #18 (The Man Who Never Goes Back)

The JACK REACHER Cases #19 (The Man From The Shadows)

The JACK REACHER CASES #20 (The Man Behind The Gun)

JACK REACHER'S SPECIAL INVESTIGATORS

BOOK ONE: DEAD MEN WALKING

BOOK TWO: GAME OVER

BOOK THREE: LIGHTS OUT

BOOK FOUR: NEVER FORGIVE, NEVER FORGET

BOOK FIVE: HIT THEM FAST, HIT THEM HARD

BOOK SIX: FINISH THE FIGHT

THE JOHN ROCKNE MYSTERIES

DEAD WOOD (John Rockne Mystery #1)

HARD ROCK (John Rockne Mystery #2)

COLD JADE (John Rockne Mystery #3)

LONG SHOT (John Rockne Mystery #4)

EASY PREY (John Rockne Mystery #5)

BODY BLOW (John Rockne Mystery #6)

THE WADE CARVER THRILLERS

MOLLY (Wade Carver Thriller #1)

SUGAR (Wade Carver Thriller #2)

ANGEL (Wade Carver Thriller #3)

THE WALLACE MACK THRILLERS

THE KILLING LEAGUE (Wallace Mack Thriller #1)

THE MURDER STORE (Wallace Mack Thriller #2)

FINDERS KILLERS (Wallace Mack Thriller #3)

THE MARY COOPER MYSTERIES

DEATH BY SARCASM (Mary Cooper Mystery #1)

MURDER WITH SARCASTIC INTENT (Mary Cooper Mystery #2)

GROSS SARCASTIC HOMICIDE (Mary Cooper Mystery #3)

THE CIRCUIT RIDER (WESTERNS)

THE CIRCUIT RIDER (Circuit Rider #1)
KILLER'S DRAW (Circuit Rider #2)

THE RAY MITCHELL THRILLERS

THE RECRUITER

KILLING THE RAT

HEAD SHOT

STANDALONE THRILLERS:

KILLER GROOVE (Rockne & Cooper Mystery #1)

BEER MONEY (Burr Ashland Mystery #1)

TO FIND A MOUNTAIN (A WWII Thriller)

BOX SETS:

AMES TO KILL
GROSSE POINTE PULP
GROSSE POINTE PULP 2
TOTAL SARCASM
WALLACE MACK THRILLER COLLECTION

SHORT STORIES:

THE GARBAGE COLLECTOR
BULLET RIVER
SCHOOL GIRL
HANGING CURVE
SCALE OF JUSTICE

Free Books And More

**Would you like a FREE copy
of my story BULLET RIVER and the chance
to win a free Kindle?**

Then sign up for the DAN AMES BOOK CLUB:

For special offers and new releases, sign up here

A USA TODAY BESTSELLING AUTHOR

LIGHTS OUT
SET IN THE REACHER UNIVERSE BY PERMISSION OF LEE CHILD

DAN AMES

A USA TODAY
BESTSELLING BOOK

Book One in The JACK REACHER Cases

CLICK HERE TO BUY NOW

Free Books And More

Would you like a FREE copy of my story BULLET RIVER and the chance to win a free Kindle?

Then sign up for the DAN AMES BOOK CLUB:

For special offers and new releases, sign up here

Praise for Dan Ames

"Fast-paced, engaging, original."

> New York TIMES BESTSELLING AUTHOR Thomas Perry

"Ames is a sensation among readers who love fast-paced thrillers."

> MYSTERY TRIBUNE

"Cuts like a knife."

> Savannah Morning News

"Furiously paced. Great action."

> New York TIMES BESTSELLING AUTHOR Ben Lieberman

LIGHTS OUT

Jack Reacher's Special Investigators

BOOK THREE

by

Dan Ames

"Never is there any law more just
than that
he who has plotted death
shall perish by his own plot."

-Ovid

Chapter 1

He knew he was dying.

It was most likely a certainty, which was a bit of an oxymoron.

Yet, it was the only explanation.

He couldn't focus and focusing had always been his strongest suit. With that gone, well, he figured that was the final push that would take him over the edge to the long, dark fall.

Ever since he was a child, solving incredibly complex math problems, acing science exams, debating chemistry issues with professors thirty years his elder, people had always remarked on his focus. His laser-like intensity.

They said it was preternatural, a talent as rare as pure genius.

Now, none of that mattered because he was truly at a loss.

Dazed.

Utterly and hopelessly confused. It was like once in college when he'd tried pot, the first and last time. A dizziness without pleasure, an unspooling of logic and awareness savored by some, but utterly distasteful to him.

Now, he stood facing the lake. It was mostly ice at this time of year, although it was still occasionally warm enough to reveal pockets of open water. The kind that swallow up an ice fisherman once every few years. He stumbled through the calculations in his head: oxygen, temperatures, theories of hydrogen and atmospheric pressure. Normally, the process would have occurred with the silky precision of a Porsche engine. Now, it was like an old clunker with thick oil chilled by cold, struggling to find a spark.

And then it was gone and he stood there with a head full of unfocused thoughts.

It must be a brain aneurysm, he thought. Was it even possible for the human brain to recognize a brain aneurysm?

The thought of his gray matter made him stand a little straighter, his eyes focused, his pupils sharpened.

The brain.

It was something he was fascinated with and had been devoting more and more time to, especially considering the experiments.

The things he'd discovered.

The thoughts fluttered around his head like the first snowflakes portending a coming blizzard.

He looked down at the ice and water, the thin patches of swirling snow.

It was very, very cold.

A human being venturing into that kind of cold would die of hypothermia very quickly. He ran the calculations in his head: body temperature, air temperature, water temperature. He thought of the experiments done by the Nazis back in World War II and then wondered why he thought of them. Was he one?

No, that was too far back in history. He wasn't that old, was he? It didn't really matter because if he went in the water he wouldn't last long. That much he knew.

He would be dead within thirty minutes, tops. Although that really wasn't the plan, was it?

What was the plan?

It had been a good one, but he kept forgetting the steps he'd put in place.

He looked down.

His shoe was an Allen-Edmonds. Very nice. Two hundred bucks. Each shoe.

He smiled.

His wife, if he had one, would have enjoyed that.

Well, that would never happen.

He took a deep breath.
And stepped into the water.

Chapter 2

They couldn't find the body.

That was one thing, and it happened all the time. So many crime scenes over the years where you knew someone had been killed but without a body, well, it was much harder to convict. Which is why smart criminals went out of their way to make sure physical evidence was destroyed permanently.

Still, the lack of a body wasn't what really bothered Detective Alex Yates of Chicago PD.

It was the vehicle.

More specifically, the witness who said the vehicle hadn't been in the same place when he'd first seen, supposedly before and then after, the man had disappeared. Ordinarily, Yates might write the detail off as a case of mistaken memory.

How many people remembered the positions of parked cars?

But this witness was different.

With a story that was totally believable.

Yates looked out at the frozen entity of Lake Michigan. This time of year it could get brutally cold in Chicago, although not as bad as the heart of winter, say, the dead middle of February. That was brutal. Like being in a frozen hell and trying to gut it out until mid-March when the first warm wind would blow in and turn the dirty snow to mush.

Right now, the lake was mostly a flat white desert of sheer ice coated with a dusting of snow, whipped into occasional drifts created by ever-shifting winds. Sporadically, in the distance, Yates could see what might be a few patches of open water. Those would close soon, like the summer cottages in northern Wisconsin after the tourists had left.

Yates stood on the cement seawall, looking at the footprints in the snow. They were going to have to make sure to get plaster casts of the tread patterns, size and detail of each impression. It was a mess, really. Multiple footprints, different sizes, all shuffled together.

But it was clear that someone most likely parked a vehicle, walked down the steep embankment to the seawall, then climbed into the water and committed suicide.

It was shallow here, and not much current.

So even though he was preoccupied a bit by the witness's testimony regarding the location of the car, Yates was nonetheless also bothered by the lack of a body. Barely two feet of water with no current? The suicide victim ought to be staring back up at them through the ice, a look of either horror or quiet satisfaction on their lifeless face.

Chicago's search and rescue team was on the way. A helicopter had already flown over utilizing the last bit of daylight, but it was no use. They couldn't see through the ice and now it was dark.

Yates had run the plate of the vehicle in question and it had come back registered to a man named James Fenton.

"He would never, ever commit suicide," Fenton's family, if he had any, would probably say. Yates knew he sounded cynical, but it was always the same. "We just saw him last week and he said he had never been happier, that he was in a great place. He was happy."

Yates had heard the same thing said many times of suicide victims. They seemed so happy was a common statement said just after a loved one disappeared. And then the whole secret life would be revealed; maybe drugs, drinking, addiction, gambling debts, an affair, a mental illness teetering on disaster.

It always came down to how well did anyone really know anyone?

"Why would he have gassed up his car just before he committed suicide?" Yates asked himself. There was a receipt in Fenton's car, showing a thirty-five dollar gas charge at a Shell station six blocks away.

That was the third thing that bothered Yates.

Why would a person who was going to kill themselves fill up their vehicle with gas? Certainty, if they were going to park in the garage and poison themselves with carbon monoxide, sure, that would make perfect sense.

But to fill up and then walk into Lake Michigan and ostensibly drown yourself?

Maybe he hadn't been sure which method to use to off himself. So he gassed up the vehicle just in case he wanted to park in the garage and leave the car running. And then ultimately, he'd decided to walk into Lake Michigan and drown himself in ice-cold water.

So that's what he had. A missing body. A gas receipt, and a witness who said the vehicle had been moved, supposedly after Fenton had killed himself.

According to an eyewitness who had walked their dog along the seawall—a husky who loved the cold—the vehicle had been parked nearly twenty feet further east. The dog walker knew this because there was a plastic bag dispenser and trash receptacle as it was a popular path for dog walkers. The dog walker had remembered that the vehicle was parked nearly in front of the trash receptacle when he walked out, and on his return, the vehicle was parked well before it. And the dog walker had grabbed a plastic bag on his way past and then dumped it in the trash on his way back.

So he was a very credible witness.

The question was, if James Fenton had parked his vehicle and walked into the freezing waters of Lake Michigan and died, who had moved the vehicle?

Chapter 3

Reacher said nothing.

The big hound sat, his eyes refusing to leave their laser-like focus on his owner; one Frances L. Neagley.

Neagley looked at her dog. He was big, muscular and of a dubious pedigree. Not a purebred, certainly, but he was a handsome animal. Intelligent. Loyal. She'd rescued him a few months earlier, and they were mostly inseparable.

Neagley was a partner in the largest and most successful private security firm in Chicago, so she did spend a fair amount of time at the office downtown. In those instances, she sometimes brought Reacher, or if it was going to be a long day at work, she would arrange a trusted neighbor to walk Reacher around noon.

The bond between owner and dog was

intense, and Neagley appreciated that aspect of her life.

The relationship worked mostly because Reacher knew to do as he was ordered, the hallmark of any good dog, or soldier.

Neagley had named the hound after her former commanding officer, Jack Reacher. Reacher had been her commanding officer when she was a military policewoman in the Army. Together, they had made a formidable team. Neagley had never known a man like Reacher and had never known one like him since.

Hence, the perfect name for the dog.

"Good boy," she said and handed him a treat: a rawhide intertwined with buffalo jerky. Neagley had been amazed by the variety of products offered in the pet world. She'd always thought it was a few kinds of milk bones and that was it.

Boy, was she wrong. She could have spent way more than she did on Reacher's stuff, and as it was, she'd spent quite a bit.

Now, she left Reacher to do his own thing.

She went into her home office and checked her email. Neagley didn't differentiate between work and personal life. She had one email, the one associated with her company. After she'd left the Army, she'd gone into private security and after working for years and being frustrated by a void in leadership at nearly every company she'd worked at, she decided to form her own company.

Her firm had been a success and was now one of the global leaders in private security.

Frances Neagley was a very wealthy woman.

She scanned through the emails, answering only the ones that really needed a response, and either deleting or filing the rest.

With that done, she booted up her preferred website for the local Chicago news. There was a live feed concerning a missing person. As Neagley watched, she saw a sliver of frozen Lake Michigan, being illuminated by red and blue police flashers, behind the reporter, who stood facing the camera, her breath a visible cloud that grew with each word.

"As of right now, there are recovery efforts underway, but the body of James Fenton has still not been found," the reporter said. She was wearing a parka with the hood up and her face looked like she was peering out of a fur-lined cave.

Neagley sat back in her chair.

James Fenton?

Why did that name sound familiar?

As she thought, a memory flashed through her consciousness, and she audibly gasped.

Could it be *that* James Fenton?

Chapter 4

Heavy rain lashed at the windshield and Edgar Chavez heard the wind roaring in from the south.

Hurricane Sebastian was a latecomer to the party; most tropical storms were over by this time of year, but Sebastian had decided to be fashionably late.

Chavez wasn't worried. He'd lived in Venice, Florida, ever since he'd gotten out of the Army, over a decade ago, and he'd seen his share of storms. A few of them had been bad and had actually resulted in the loss of significant lives. However, they were the rarity. Most hurricanes just caused a certain level of inconvenience: a lack of power, flooding, debris, and plenty of traffic issues. But when you lived in Florida, it's what you expected so most people didn't complain.

Still, this late in the season, a hurricane was

rare. At least Sebastian's eye was staying off the coast of Florida - some fifty miles away, but sometimes the wind on the outskirts of the storm did more damage than those more powerful gusts near the eye. In Chavez's experiences, hurricanes had a way of giving one false hope. Every time a weather reporter claimed a hurricane's movement was positive, there was always a negative counterpart.

A part of Chavez enjoyed seeing the onset of a good storm. They were subtle reminders that human beings weren't really in control.

While the storm wasn't causing Chavez any stress, an odd message from one of his clients was.

Edgar Chavez was CEO of a cyber security consulting firm. Although his company was small, he had clients all over the world. He was in high enough demand that he kept his clientele limited enough to ensure he had eyes on nearly every project. With a small staff in Venice, he also kept freelancers in various parts of the world, with specialties that he sometimes needed.

The client who had reached out to him earlier was a rare local; a woman with a small catering company who had asked for computer security after she'd been stalked by a former customer.

Chavez had been suggested by a mutual friend and although her budget was a fraction of what he would normally charge, he helped her out and was even invited to her wedding. Her husband worked as a fish and game warden in the greater Tampa area, just north of Venice.

The woman's name was Dorothy Greer, and her missing husband's name was Thomas. According to Dorothy, Thomas had left work the evening before and never made it home. Frantic calls to the fish and game office had yielded nothing, and Dorothy knew of Chavez's background as an investigator with the military police in the Army.

An hour earlier, Dorothy had contacted him, telling Chavez that Thomas's truck had been found south of Sarasota and to the east - in a vast area of state land, mostly swamp.

Chavez's Range Rover was equipped with all-wheel drive, which he usually didn't need in Florida, but heading into state swampland in the middle of a hurricane made him glad he had it.

It took him an hour to reach the scene where the truck was found.

There were several cops there, as well as a crime scene unit. The wind was whipping, and rain lashed at everyone. The cops had on dark slickers, and Chavez put on his wide-brimmed bush hat.

Chavez recognized one of the cops - he'd gotten to know quite a few of the Venice and

Sarasota cops, and this guy had a condo a few doors down from Chavez. His name was Avila.

Chavez caught his eye and nodded toward an area behind the investigators.

"What are you doing out here?" Avila asked.

"I did some work for the missing guy's wife. She's worried."

Avila winced and Chavez knew exactly what he meant.

"He's dead?"

Avila glanced around to make sure no one was listening.

"Yeah, and then some."

"Accident?"

Avila shook his head. Chavez recognized his friend's reticence. Something was wrong.

"Jesus, what happened?"

"I've never seen anything like it."

Chavez waited until Avila finally let out a long breath and spoke.

"The bastards skinned him alive."

Chapter 5

The nerd.

That's how Neagley remembered James Fenton. It had been many years ago, when Neagley was an MP in the Army. There'd been one of those brilliant bureaucratic brainstorms: let's assemble a group of way too many people and spend way too much time mucking about without a clear directive and chain of command.

If her memory served her right, Fenton had been a computer nerd. She remembered him because first, she had a great recall when it came to names and faces from her past.

Secondly, it was because he had reminded her of a Christmas elf. Fenton had been short, slight, with a little wispy blond hair and bright blue eyes along with a cherubic face. In short, a cross between a computer geek and one of Santa's elves. Neagley had amused herself by thinking that instead of working on the computer, he was assembling it as a gift for a child somewhere.

Despite his amusing appearance, Neagley couldn't deny that he was seriously talented.

The case had been interesting: a serial rapist had been assaulting young Iraqi women and leaving false clues to pin the attacks on the occupying American soldiers. Neagley had been part of the team to investigate the attacks and it was clear no Americans were in the area at most of the times and locations of the crimes.

So the job had been to figure out who among the Iraqi civilians was the guilty party.

But while the people in charge had been getting nothing done, James Fenton had written an algorithm studying the times, locations and methods of the attack, as well as the data already gathered in the investigations. Soon, he had zeroed in on an interesting angle: whomever was doing the attacks always knew where the Americans *weren't* going to be. Fenton then analyzed the data of civilian contractors with any history of crimes against women and soon came up with one man.

Neagley and her team tracked him down and found him with multiple souvenirs of his rapes. The man had been arrested, turned over to local Iraqi authorities, who had promptly executed him.

The task force had been quietly disassembled and everyone had gone their separate ways.

She'd never seen Fenton again, but had always remembered his quiet intelligence and the fact that he'd saved probably dozens more women from being raped.

And now he'd just walked into Lake Michigan and drowned himself?

Neagley didn't believe it.

She thought for a moment about who she knew at Chicago PD and picked up the phone.

Chapter 6

"It will never work."

The slender Asian man with a slight overbite grinned. His name was Avan Luu and his dark eyes were full of merriment; he was enjoying this moment. Dashing the dreams of others had always been one of his favorite pastimes. His petite frame was draped in an expensive suit and his dark glasses were from Europe. He looked more like a corporate trader than a Chinese gangster.

The other man on the pier overlooking Lake Michigan was Luu's opposite: Henry Mah was short and compact. His suit was off the rack and he rarely smiled. Completely out of place in his wardrobe was the gold and diamond Rolex he wore on his wrist.

"Why do you say that?" Mah replied.

Luu flashed his oversized front teeth. "Because I control the remaining groups and we have no intention of unifying. Any cut in our revenue is a cut. Subtraction. Plain and simple."

"A smaller cut of a larger pie is not less. It's more. Addition."

Mah didn't smile. His face was like overbaked terra cotta and his mode of expression was always the same: neutral tinged by a thin veil of contempt.

Luu stopped smiling. "Your ambition has always been your strong suit, Henry. Unfortunately, you should have talked to me before you began this lofty goal. I certainly would have advised you against mounting the undertaking and saved you considerable resources in the process. Sometimes, a streak of independence is actually a losing streak in its infancy."

"Perhaps I saved the best for last, as the Americans say," Mah replied, refusing to take the bait. He'd played games like these hundreds of time. By his own reckoning, he had yet to lose.

"I've watched you spend exorbitant amounts of time, money and effort pulling together the most powerful Chinese syndicates in the U.S.," Luu said. His voice had become lower, more forceful. "But alas, planning isn't your strong suit. You should have begun with me, not ended with me. I didn't choose to be the undertaker to your dreams, but it is a job I can perform with ease."

Mah looked over Luu's shoulder. The moon was nearly full, its reflection bobbed and swayed among the gentle waves of the lake. It was a beautiful night, Mah thought.

In fact, it was perfect.

The dagger possessed a traditional Chinese form, however, the metal was the best the 21st century technology had to offer. Mah slid it with practiced ease from its concealed scabbard in his sleeve and he thrust it with power and precision. The beautifully honed blade cut with ease into the flesh of Luu's abdomen and as Mah thrust upward, it sliced effortlessly through internal organs. Hot blood gushed onto Mah's hand and he stepped back to ensure none would spoil the cloth of his suit. He hadn't paid as much as Luu had for his, but Mah didn't believe in wasting money.

This turned out to be one of those rare occasions that caused Mah to smile. His perfect teeth caught the glint of the moonlight overhead, and behind him, he heard his bodyguards fire their silenced weapons into the bodies of Luu's security men.

Mah leaned in toward Luu's face. He whispered.

"What did you say about my ability to plan?" he asked.

Luu gurgled blood.

Mah stepped back, pulled the dagger out of his adversary's chest, and pushed Luu backward off the dock into the water. He used a handkerchief to wipe his prints from the dagger and then tossed that into the lake. It was a beautiful weapon, but he had half a dozen more just like it back in his home.

He turned, saw his men waiting for him by his custom Rolls Royce with tinted, bulletproof windows.

Mah walked toward them and held out his hand.

His top security man, a brooding hulk named Ip, handed him a cell phone.

Mah slid into the back seat of the Rolls and punched in a number.

"Have you found him yet?" he asked.

Chapter 7

He stared at his toes.

They were beyond pale, almost translucent. His feet were alabaster, save for a few scraggly hairs here and there. Set against the backdrop of the dark blue carpet, they almost looked like alien creatures, or pieces of plastic missed by the cleaning lady.

James Fenton was fascinated. It also occurred to him that he had no idea where his socks were. That thought was followed to its natural progression: *where were his shoes?*

His mind, a paragon of analytical thinking, recognized that he was in a hotel room. And for James Fenton, he with no family and very little spare time, that almost certainly meant a business trip. He'd probably flown here for a meeting and checked into the hotel. Maybe he'd fallen asleep before he was able to get fully undressed.

The problem was, he usually chose only the finest accommodations. Large, upscale hotels with a nice restaurant attached, a gym and pool, valet parking.

This room was a dump. The dark blue carpet was dirty, the paint on the walls was peeling, and the dropped ceiling tiles had patches of brown water damage. It smelled like a wet cat and somewhere, some kind of machinery was clanking as if it were in its death throes.

A business trip? Fenton wondered. *Then why had his secretary booked him into such a crap hotel?*

He thought about what it would mean if he wasn't here on business. Why would he be in this hotel on his own? Had he met someone at a bar? Picked up a woman and she'd brought him here?

That didn't make sense. He hadn't dated anyone in years and sex wasn't all that much a priority for him. What turned him on were computer codes and algorithms.

Hookers and cheap hotels? Not so much.

Fenton walked back to the bed – a twin mattress with a threadbare sheet and one moldy pillow. He noticed a pair of socks and shoes next to it. He reached down and touched them.

They were sopping wet.

He also recognized them: they were his.

His mind stuttered and stopped and started again. Images of a large body of water, flashes of a vehicle, men, and the sense that he needed to hide.

Hide from what?

It was like trying to remember someone's name that was just on the fringe of your memory. There was a reason he was here in this room. There was a reason his shoes and socks were wet.

And there was a reason he wasn't calling the police.

It was because there was one overriding emotion that he did, indeed, recognize.

Fear.

Chapter 8

Like any big city, among practitioners of a certain industry, Chicago could feel like a small town. Cops, and to an even more intense degree, homicide detectives, would agree.

Frances Neagley had spent the better part of a decade working at and then owning the most prestigious private security firm in Chicago. Over the years, she had gotten to know most of the detectives in the Windy City, and Alex Yates was no exception.

She didn't know him well, mostly by reputation. And that reputation was sketchy.

Still, she managed to get his cell phone number, called him and they agreed to meet for a cup of coffee on her dime.

The place was a diner not far from the homicide offices downtown.

Yates was sitting at the counter and Neagley recognized him from the door. Her cop radar never failed her. Yates was an average-looking man, the kind of guy who probably played sports but never managed to be a starter on any of his teams. And then when middle age arrived, he'd slid into it without much thought of fighting to retain his youth, which hadn't been all that great to begin with.

She slid onto the stool next to him and ordered a coffee.

"Thanks for meeting with me," she said.

"I heard it was a smarter move than turning you down," Yates replied evenly. She knew exactly what he meant: over the years, Neagley and her firm had employed many ex-detectives, some of whom still retained a lot of clout within the organization. Yates was telling her that he was here in no small part because he felt she could hurt his career if she so chose.

While she didn't think she had that much power, there was some truth in that line of thought, she supposed. She probably could do some damage if she really wanted to, but she would never think of doing so, unless the circumstances were extremely dire.

"Just a friendly chat about James Fenton," Neagley said.

"That's what I figured."

The server brought Neagley's coffee, black, and placed it in front of her.

"Have you ordered?" Neagley asked Yates.

"Egg white omelet," he said, without the slightest trace of enthusiasm. "Trying to lose a few pounds."

The server, a young man with a goatee, glanced at Neagley but she shook her head.

"What's your interest in Fenton?" Yates asked.

"We worked together as part of a team back when I was in the Army."

"I didn't know you were Army," Yates said. "What did you do?"

"Military police."

"Makes sense. What did Fenton do?"

Neagley hesitated. She figured Yates already knew but wanted to hear what she knew first. It was smart. It's probably what she would have done.

"It was one of those joint task forces," Neagley answered. "Fenton was some branch of intelligence, I'm not sure which one. But it was a case involving a serial rapist and Fenton knocked it out of the park. He basically caught the perp single-handedly and put an end to some really bad stuff."

If Yates knew all this, he played his cards close to the vest.

"He was quiet, did his job brilliantly and then

I never saw him again," Neagley continued. "So when I saw on the news he'd possibly disappeared under somewhat strange circumstances, I felt like I owed him to at least ask a couple of questions."

"That kind of a military code thing?" Yates asked.

Neagley didn't bother answering.

"So what do you want to know?"

"Foul play?"

Yates sighed. "Too early. But no one saw him go in the water. The only witness was a dog walker who said the car was in a different position in the time between Fenton supposedly decided to take a dip."

Neagley immediately saw the implications.

"If Fenton wanted to bail on his life and fake his death, he wouldn't have moved his vehicle twice."

"Unless he wanted to make us all think he was murdered."

"Or maybe he was murdered."

Yates lifted up his hands as if to say, of course.

"Any signs of life in his financials?"

Oftentimes, a missing person's credit card or debit card would see activity and lead authorities to their whereabouts.

"Nada," Yates answered. "Except he gassed up his vehicle just before his swim lesson. Kind of odd for a suicide."

"Yeah, that's a new one," Neagley said. "So where do you think this thing is going?"

"You didn't hear this from me," Yates said. He looked at Neagley, and she hid her frustration at the implied insult that she needed to be told to keep things confidential. She was always discreet and honored her sources, and if Yates had done his homework, he would've known that, too.

Yates glanced around the diner as if he wanted to make sure no one was listening, and then he leaned in toward Neagley.

"Whatever this guy did for a living? We can't find it. He's a goddamned ghost."

Chapter 9

Edgar Chavez was no stranger to dealing with families of recently murdered individuals. As an MP in the Army, he'd had to do it many times. Working under Jack Reacher, Chavez had seen the best way to deal with it: straight ahead, no beating around the bush. That only made it worse and the families deserved better.

As it turned out, he didn't have to worry about how to break the news.

Chavez had been to the Greers' house only once, briefly for a quick meeting with Dorothy regarding her case. It was a low slung Florida ranch, probably built in the fifties. It had beige aluminum siding with green trim. The landscaping was simple and neat.

There were three cars parked in the driveway, one of which Chavez recognized as Dorothy's.

LIGHTS OUT

When he rang the bell on the front door and Dorothy opened it, Chavez knew immediately she'd already been notified. She was a short, dark woman, but he'd always known her to be upbeat and energetic. The woman who answered the door was the complete opposite. In shock, full of despair, and robbed of her life's energy.

Chavez wondered how many details she'd been given about her husband's murder. Hopefully, not many.

"Oh, Edgar," she said. He hugged her and then stepped into the room and saw there were two other people standing awkwardly in the living room: one of them was clearly Dorothy's sister as they almost appeared to be twins. The brother-in-law was a tall, thin man with thick glasses, jeans and a sweater vest. He looked like a community college professor.

"This is my sister and her husband," Dorothy said.

They nodded to Edgar and Dorothy's sister handed her a mug of tea.

"I'm so sorry," Edgar said to the group.

Dorothy brought Edgar up to speed. The detectives had paid her a visit, told her about Thomas and had been asked the requisite questions. Afterward, Dorothy's sister had arrived and together, they had begun to make the necessary arrangements.

"I don't understand it," she said. "Thomas was loved by everyone. He was everyone's friend. Who would want to do this to him?" Her face cracked and she began to sob. Dorothy's sister put her arms around her shoulders and the sister's husband went to make more tea.

"I know the detectives," Chavez said. "They'll do a good job."

"I know," Dorothy said. "But I want you to work on it, too."

Chavez winced inwardly. The local cops were good, but they wouldn't appreciate a local investigator sticking his nose in where they felt it didn't belong. Besides, at this point in his career, computer crimes were his forte.

Although, his background as one of Jack Reacher's special investigators was something that belonged to him deep in his marrow.

It was something that would never leave him.

"I don't understand," Chavez said.

Dorothy turned and walked down the hall. Moments later, she returned with a laptop.

"This was Tom's personal computer, not the one he used at work. The cops didn't ask for it, and I'm no good with technology. Why don't you go through it and see if you can find anything that might help catch whoever did this to my husband. Computers are your thing, right?"

Chavez started to protest.

She held up a hand.

"You don't have to investigate, but if you find something, maybe you can send it to the detectives in charge and they can use it.

Chavez reluctantly took the computer.

"Okay," he said.

Chapter 10

It wasn't that Henry Mah thought he was a modern-age Sun Tzu, the famous Chinese philosopher and author of the legendary *The Art of War*. It was that Mah thought he was *better* than Sun Tzu.

Smarter.

More ruthless.

Which is why Mah was now watching his men organizing their armaments. It was one thing to execute a rival. It was quite another to take over the dead man's businesses and convince leftover employees that they now needed to pledge their loyalty to the new boss.

If history had taught Mah anything, and Mah was a fervent student of the past, it was that a good many of those people would refuse to shift their allegiances. In some cases, Mah predicted fifty percent. They would, of course, be summarily executed.

The first death, which would be the most gruesome and painful to watch, often drove up the number of converts.

Mah's headquarters were located in a mixed-use commercial area a mile from the freeway and less than ten minutes from O'Hare Airport. The centerpiece of the complex was a towering corporate office of steel and glass. Mah owned the entire top floor.

Next door to the office building was a trucking warehouse which was also one hundred percent owned by Mah. It was here that he kept his men, weapons and vehicles. Control was very important to him, and Mah relished the fact he could look out of his office windows and see the warehouse.

It made his men work a little harder, a little more efficiently, and quite a bit more loyally, knowing he was watching.

One of Mah's favorite quotes, paraphrased, from Sun Tzu was *"…a clever fighter not only wins… but wins with ease…"*

So far, his consolidation of power had not been terribly difficult. No one had been able to do it for at least a century: engineer the unification of all the Chinese triads and gangs into one cohesive crime syndicate.

Mah had just completed that process on paper

with the murder of Luu. Now, he had to make it a reality on the street.

He signaled for his next in command, Ip, to gather the men.

Mah waited for his lieutenants to assemble.

"You've each been given a region to command," he said. "You will lead as I have led. You will be an extension of my rule."

The men had already been given their marching orders, but Mah wanted to be clear.

"Failure is not an option. Nor is mercy," he continued. "There is no room within this new organization for a single misstep. The world is watching."

A dozen black vans roared into the space, and the men loaded their weapons into the vehicles.

After they'd left, Mah returned to his office.

Like any military general, and that's what Mah considered himself, he kept the overall battle plan to himself, and a few trusted individuals back in Beijing. Among his men here, he was the only one able to see the big picture.

Consolidating the various groups was only phase one and not even the most important.

No, what was happening elsewhere was much more crucial to Mah's success both in the U.S. and back in his homeland China.

Mah retreated to the personal apartment he kept behind secure doors on the tenth floor. It was an opulent suite full of expensive artwork and several young women.

They were his employees, and their only job was to guarantee his pleasure in their presence.

He walked into his bedroom, took off his clothes and placed a small black box on the night table. He might use it tonight, or he might not.

Fully naked, he called the women into the bedroom and allowed them to do their work.

Chapter 11

Washington, D.C.

THE NAME he went by these days was Galleon. It bore no resemblance to his real name which was whispered in elite circles around Boston, D.C. and Palm Beach. His birth name had served him well and as a youth had helped him gain entrée into the rarified air of Yale, the Skull & Bones Society, and a plethora of political connection that made his entrance into the intelligence community a formality.

Galleon was not currently happy. In fact, he was angry in the smoldering sense: a fire had been lit and no one had lifted a finger to stop it. And now, it was creating the kind of smoke that was noticeable by the people whom Galleon did not want to be noticed.

The operation was both simple and complex. Simple in the sense that it had only a few moving parts; complex because the individual players were responsible for executing their portion of the endeavor and so far, multiple failures had occurred.

Galleon did not care for failure. Also, he refused to accept it.

He called in his assistant. Although this office was not their official abode, it was luxurious nonetheless. An outrageous monthly rent and the best in purchased furniture made the space seem even more powerful and intimidating than he'd perhaps intended. It was a sideline, this operation, and he wanted distance from his actual, sanctioned activities back along the Potomac.

His assistant's name was Kaye and she was petite, redheaded and a hundred times more vicious than Galleon. Next to his patrician good looks and powerful frame, they made a striking and dangerous pair.

"Please tell me you've found him," Galleon said.

"Not yet," Kaye said. Her pale face was pinched, her mouth set in a firm line. To most men, she would be fairly attractive, but Galleon knew too much about her and had too much shared experience with her to have those feelings. To him, she was like a shark constantly circling, waiting to tear into innocent flesh.

It was why he'd chosen her to be his number two.

"Any ideas?" he asked.

"No one's looking at the money, or more accurately, for the money," Kaye responded. "As long as they're focused on other things, we have time to nip this thing in the bud."

Galleon was still thinking of the shark analogy.

Especially in terms of if this whole thing went off the rails.

How he would be able to put all the blame on Kaye.

He imagined pushing her head underwater, and then he wondered if, in the process, she would bite off his arm.

Chapter 12

He's a goddamned ghost, Yates had said.

Neagley didn't believe in ghosts. Oh, she thought people were haunted by their actions, past sins, and choices made or not made. But true ghosts? No way.

Plus, she'd met James Fenton in the flesh and knew he was as real as a heart attack. He was no apparition, and his line of work wasn't something mystical.

Fenton had been in the intelligence community, a whiz with computers and software. Plus, she'd remembered his physical appearance: one of Santa's elves that left the toy factory and went into the American intelligence community.

Neagley had already taken Reacher for a long walk, and now he was snoozing in front of the fireplace. She went to her home office and fired up her computer, which was also linked with her workstation at the office, meaning all of the databases and private security access were enabled for her at home, too. She worked so much and kept such odd hours that it had been a mandatory situation, even though the IT team had initially objected. For security reasons, of course. But those had been thoroughly addressed and now she could work from home with the same level of protection as her office downtown.

Now, she booted up the Department of Defense's internal website and logged in. She'd earned access to it long ago and had managed to maintain it even though she was no longer in the military. It was because she had become an official vendor of the Pentagon. Once in, she had taken some liberties with passwords and servers to get access to the kinds of records her job demanded.

James Fenton appeared in several folders.

She attacked them chronologically, and it quickly became apparent that Fenton had originally been an analyst with the CIA. Neagley had been able to determine this by codes used in his employee number—she'd long ago memorized which codes represented specific branches of the military.

She was also able to determine that he had risen quickly—his pay grade had repeatedly been raised over his first four years at Langley.

And then he'd disappeared.

Wiped from the personnel records.

This would have been just after he'd worked with Neagley on the joint task force overseas. Probably when he'd rotated back to the U.S.

So where had he gone?

To answer the question, Neagley opened the next two folders.

One of the mentions was meaningless: a summit on some environmental issue, which Neagley figured might have been a typo or a different James Fenton.

The final instance of Fenton's paper trail was an incident report deemed classified.

Neagley sat back in her chair. She knew all too well what that terminology meant: someone had implicated Fenton in a possibly illegal activity. Incident reports of this type could range from theft to sexual assault to drug use.

The implications were immediate. The James Fenton she remembered didn't seem like the type, but then again, Neagley had met and witnessed much evil perpetrated by perfectly innocent seeming individuals.

Unfortunately, Neagley's access did not allow her to gain entry into the classified report, and even her friend and former colleague Edgar Chavez, who was a genius when it came to computers, probably couldn't, and more importantly, wouldn't *want* to break into classified servers at the Department of Defense.

No, she would have to simply wait on that incident report and see if there was another way to go about finding out what may or may not have happened.

Because Neagley was not new to investigations, and her instinct had been well honed over the years, something told her that whatever that incident report involved, it probably had something to do with this current disappearance.

She closed the window on her computer and decided to go and check on Reacher.

In the morning, she wanted to take a firsthand look at where Fenton lived and who might have known him personally.

She had a feeling the answer would be no one.

Chapter 13

The computer was the typical Costco special: a cheap PC with a fair amount of memory and a basic processor. Edgar Chavez studied the home screen, not surprised that Thomas Greer had virtually no security on the machine. It was a personal computer after all, and Greer must have felt that there was no need to enable a password to get into the machine or to encrypt any of the information on the hard drive. If he only used it at home, why would he need to create some kind of elaborate log in system if the only other person who might be near it was his wife?

It became rapidly apparent to Chavez that Thomas Greer had not been much of a desk jockey. There were only a few folders on the computer, and most of them were personal; things like birthday pictures, family contact information and an internet history almost exclusively dealing with fishing and hunting.

Greer, before being skinned alive in the Florida swamp, had been a mid-level fish and game officer. It seemed that he enjoyed what he did and took it seriously. He'd been with the organization for over ten years and had been promoted several times.

Chavez noted that Greer had bookmarked several law enforcement sites, including the FBI. In one of the folders, Chavez found Greer's resume along with several letters and applications to the FBI.

It appeared that Greer had always wanted to be a G-man but had never been accepted.

Chavez sped through the hard drive, looking for any signs of hidden data or indications that the computer had been hacked. Perhaps the people who had killed Greer had also infiltrated his computer, but Chavez saw no such evidence.

It did seem that Greer's real passion was fishing, because he had a dozen folders each labeled by a specific species. Chavez saw that Greer had also been certified as a diver and wondered if he'd been a shark tooth hunter, a popular pastime especially in the Venice Beach area.

With the entire contents of the computer searched, Chavez copied it all onto his computer system for further study.

Chavez set the computer aside and thought about Dorothy. He wondered how much she knew about her husband's murder.

He picked up his phone.

He needed to help her out, and to do that, he would have to reach out to Avila. Maybe they'd found something.

For Dorothy's sake, he hoped so.

Chapter 14

Home, James.

The words reverberated in his brain. Home, James. Why did he keep saying it to himself? And then it came to him, that was his name.

James.

He pictured himself behind the wheel of a car and someone jokingly saying, "Home, James."

Was it real?

Yes, the name part was. And the phrase had been said to him on more than one occasion. As a joke. As something a rich person says to their limousine driver.

His name was James.

And right now, he wanted to go home. More than anything. But where was home?

That, he didn't know.

What he did know is that it wasn't this flea-bitten hotel room. He'd had enough.

His socks were still a little damp, and his shoes felt soggy, but he put them on and left the room. He stepped outside and thought the air was chilled, the sun hit him full force. It felt warm, a relief from the cold dampness of the room.

Still, it was winter and his overcoat was thin. It, too, was damp.

He knew he couldn't spend too much time outside, and he wasn't sure if he had a car. Somewhere in the back of his brain, an image of an SUV flitted across his consciousness, but in the hotel parking lot, there were only three vehicles. All of them were cars, with visible rust, and none of them had been cleaned in ages.

No sign of an SUV.

Perhaps he had imagined it.

James crossed the parking lot and reached a sidewalk that led to an intersection. On his right was a diner and laundromat, on his left a gas station. There were a few cars on the road, but no one gave him a second glance.

He searched inside his pockets but they were empty.

Something told him movement was good. He stepped off the curb and was halfway through the intersection when a memory spiked into vision: a home and the name of a town.

Suddenly, his brain buzzed and pain shot through his neck.

He stopped, felt his knees buckle and then he turned and saw the truck, just before it ran him over.

Chapter 15

Although Yates hadn't given her a copy of the police report, Neagley had spotted an address listed as the location of Fenton's residence.

She'd loaded Reacher into the back seat of her BMW and pointed the big car west out of Chicago. The address was a little community approximately halfway between Rockford and the Windy City.

It was a pleasant drive, and the big car and its V12 engine ate up the road. The dog was sleeping in the back—Neagley had taken him for a six-mile run to make sure he was tired out for the trip.

Ordinarily, she never would have brought the big hound dog with her, but since this was a bit of surveillance, having a dog helped her blend in and discourage suspicion. How many burglars brought along their pet?

She took an exit from the freeway and soon found herself in an idyllic little town with the kind of quaint American main streets they write songs about. Neagley pulled through a picturesque downtown, with a pretty main street and historic buildings.

Beyond that, she took a couple of turns and soon pulled up in front of a modest house, a bungalow probably built in the 20s or 30s. It had a large front porch with an overhang, and a single gable dominating the front of the structure. Neagley drove past the house and parked a couple of blocks away. It was a nice neighborhood, upper middle class, she presumed. Lots of bungalows with arts and crafts touches. The occasional new construction where someone had decided to just tear down the old house instead of fixing it up.

She woke up Reacher, put him on the leash and together they walked back toward the house. Neagley saw no signs of police tape, but she was sure the detectives had already gone through the place with a fine-tooth comb. Neagley knew Yates had referred to Fenton as a ghost because of his inability to find out the man's occupation or means of living. However, this house was brick and mortar all the way, proof that Fenton had either made good money or was making a sizeable income.

She reached Fenton's house and walked up to

the front door and rang the bell. Neagley knew there would be no one there, but she also knew there was likely a neighbor watching.

She made a big deal out of looking impatient and then walked to the back door of the house, trying to peer in through the windows as she walked along. The interior was darker, though, and the exterior reflections meant she couldn't see anything. The back of the house also had a porch, smaller, with a single door. She knocked and waited, but no one answered.

Neagley took Reacher back to the front and tried to appear frustrated, which was fairly easy to do.

"Haven't seen him for a while," a voice said. She glanced to her right and saw an old man peeking his head out of the front door of the house next door. It was a bungalow similar in style to Fenton's but it didn't look as well-maintained.

"Any idea when he'll be back?" she asked.

"Nope. Cops asked the same thing."

"Cops?"

She walked toward the old man's home. Reacher stood at her side, his ears perked forward.

"Good lookin' dog," the old man said. "Had one like him myself years ago."

"Thanks. He keeps me busy."

"I bet he does just that."

Reacher's tail wagged.

"Do you want to pet him?" she asked.

The old man stepped out and shut the door behind him. He approached and stroked Reacher's head. He was the same height as Neagley and had bowed shoulders. But his eyes were blue and alert.

"My name's Ray," the old man said. "Ray Buckner."

"Nice to meet you, Ray," Neagley said and told him her name.

"You a friend of Jim's?" he asked.

"Yeah, we used to work together a long time ago. I just happened to be in the area and thought I'd stop by. What with his name being mentioned in the news."

"I told the cops Jim had a busy travel schedule with his work," Bucker said. "He could be gone for weeks. Sometimes a month would go by, and I wouldn't see him. He had a kid cut his grass in the summer and a service plows the driveway in winter."

"I would've told them the same thing," Neagley said. She wanted to build a rapport with Buckner because she had every intention of coming back to Fenton's house later, under the cover of darkness.

"They kept asking me what he did for a living, and I was kinda embarrassed to admit I didn't know," the old man said. "Something with the government, right?"

Neagley realized the old man thought she knew Fenton better than he did. "Back when I knew him he was into computers, but he never told me exactly what he did, either. We weren't in the same department and it wasn't for the government. Later, after we'd gone our separate ways, he never mentioned the government part."

"Well," the old man gave her a sly smile. "He didn't exactly tell me that. I saw his government badge once. Jim had it on the kitchen table under some papers, and it was kind of sticking out a little."

"So you saw his job title?"

"Heck no!" Buckner said. Another one of those smiles and the blue eyes twinkling. "But I figured it out—he was a truck driver, I'm pretty sure. He might have worked with computers when you knew him, but I'm pretty sure he drove a big rig."

"Really? A government truck driver?"

"Sure. How do you think the government hauls all that crap they have?" the older man said. "You know, those ten thousand dollar toilet seats they keep buying at the Pentagon."

"Did you tell the cops he was a truck driver?"

"Nah, I was just guessing sort of, and the one cop called me an old man when he thought I wasn't listening," Ray said. "I didn't care for that one bit. Although I'm a big fan of law and order, I wasn't about to help that detective do his job if he's going to mock me for my age. Why, when I was a younger man I would've whupped his ass."

Neagley nodded as if she couldn't have agreed more. "How did you manage to guess that Jim was a truck driver?'

"Easy," the old man said. "I saw OTR next to his name."

Neagley knitted her brows. "Over the road? As in over the road truck drivers?"

"Sure. They're the long haul ones. Drive freight for a few weeks at a time."

Neagley's mind shifted suddenly, and she thanked Buckner. She handed him a business card with her cell phone number listed and urged him to call her if he saw or heard anything.

"Let's go," she said to Reacher.

Neagley had remembered what OTR might stand for. And when she tried to remember where it might be located, the truth slammed home with the kind of integrity every investigator craves.

She fired up the big car and put the engine to the test.

Chapter 16

Detective Avila asked Chavez to meet him at the jetty in Venice. It was probably the most popular spot in the small community, full of people going to see the ocean and just as many to fish from the rocks.

It was the gateway to the Gulf, and game fish moved in and out of the channel quite regularly. It wasn't unheard of to catch a good-sized fish from the jetty. There had even been an eight-foot tiger shark caught in recent memory. Not something the swimmers just down the beach were too happy to hear about.

Chavez spotted the detective on a park bench, behind a row of fishermen casting lures into the middle of the channel. Boat traffic was minimal, and the air was cool with a nice breeze coming inland from the water.

"Hey," Chavez said as he slid onto the bench next to Avila. "They catching anything?"

Avila pointed at an older man in a Superman t-shirt and cut off blue jean shorts. "Clark Kent there caught a good-sized snook a few minutes back. Threw him back in the water, though."

Chavez watched the man fish, heard a speedboat take off behind them and plunge into the bigger waves of the Gulf.

"Speaking of fish," Chavez began.

Avila held up a hand. "Look, this is all off the record. If I share anything, it's not to be repeated. And if it is and I find myself in court, I'll deny it with my last breath."

"Understood."

"So Thomas Greer was a good fish and game officer," Avila said. "Spotless record, reputation for being tough but fair. He had a real passion for conservation and law enforcement. He'd even tried to join the force here in Venice."

Chavez already knew that, and knew that Greer had even applied to join the FBI, but he didn't mention it.

"If he busted lots of folks for illegal fishing and hunting, that could have made him more than a few enemies, considering the types of folks around here," Chavez said. Southwestern Florida was known to be, like the rest of Florida, an anything goes kind of place. Plenty of stories of illegal hunting and fishing, especially when it came to alligators and deer.

"Yeah, he caught some bad guys over the years, and more than one of them made some public statements about getting revenge so we're checking it out."

"Any one more promising than others?"

"Not yet. Two of them are dead. One's in prison. And two others, we haven't been able to find. But we'll catch up with them."

"Any chance it was just a wrong-place-at-the-wrong-time kind of thing? Maybe he surprised a poacher, and it turned out in the worst way imaginable?"

"Always possible," Avila admitted. "But so far, no signs of any struggle. No forensics, really. No murder weapon. Greer was off duty, and he hadn't called anything in. We're still waiting on his cell phone records. That's our best hope, in my opinion."

Chavez was surprised Greer was off duty. What would he have been doing in the swamp? Fishing? Hunting?

"What about his coworkers, or his supervisors? Did they have any insight into what he was working on?"

"Nothing special," Avila said. "Just the usual poaching and rumors of stuff being sent overseas. They've got some strange beliefs on that side of the world when it comes to delicacies and their supposed powers."

Avila grimaced as his cell phone vibrated. He checked the screen and sighed. "That's all I can share at the moment," he said. He got up from the bench after Chavez thanked him for his help, went to his car and drove out of the jetty's gravel parking lot.

Chavez stayed where he was seated. Something was bothering him about what Avila had told him. It was just beyond his reach and it bothered him. He sat and watched the fishermen. They were getting frustrated, he could tell. No bites. No action.

Chavez lifted his gaze and looked out at the Gulf. At the huge expanse of flat blue-green glass.

A dolphin surfaced and dove, only the shape of a dorsal fin flashing for a moment.

And just like that, Chavez realized what he'd been missing.

Chapter 17

At Central Hospital of Chicago, the physician's assistant in charge of the John Doe hit-and-run car accident was a thirty-year-old African-American woman whose last name was Tilford.

She wasn't new to the job and had seen lots of trauma cases as her current rotation had her in the emergency room. The man in Room 702 was interesting for several reasons: one, he was missing any form of identification whatsoever; secondly, the nature of his injuries had caused a great deal of interest in the attending physicians.

And finally, most importantly, Tilford had seen the man's face before.

Now, she went to her desk and launched her notification folder: it was a place where high-priority messages to the hospital staff were placed, and she'd always dutifully read all the messages sent to her.

Recently, there had been a BOLO (be on the lookout) for a missing person. His name was James Fenton, and the police had supplied a photo.

Tilford found the message, opened it, and read it briefly. Then, she clicked on the photo. An image appeared full screen, probably an employment photo or maybe a better-than-average driver's license picture.

In any event, there was no doubt the unidentified patient in Room 702 was the missing James Fenton.

Tilford picked up the phone, went back to the message, and dialed the police department's phone number supplied at the bottom of the message.

Chapter 18

Galleon pressed the hidden button beneath his desk, triggering the hidden deadbolts in his office door to unlock. Shortly thereafter, Kaye entered. She had on a conservative blue business suit and her red hair, pale face and pursed lips told him all he needed to know. In most people, her appearance would seem to indicate fear or anxiety.

But Galleon knew his assistant better than that.

Kaye was excited.

"We have him," she said. She held up a piece of paper in her hand. "Central Hospital just called the Chicago PD—John Doe matching Fenton's description."

"How can we be sure?" Galleon asked. There had already been enough mistakes on this operation, one more would be the needle that broke the bureaucrat's back.

"For starters, the scene of the accident was near a cheap motel that also had a man matching Fenton's description check in the night before. Seems the man was somewhat disoriented."

"Okay…"

"Secondly, the hotel wasn't too far from where Fenton abandoned his vehicle."

"Makes sense," Galleon said, keeping his enthusiasm in check.

"Finally, I was able to get a summary of the medical report," Kaye's mouth was parting and her razor-sharp teeth seemed to gleam in the overhead light. "Seems he was hit by a car," Kaye said, her voice almost mocking in a singsong way. "Some of the injuries were consistent with blunt force trauma from a vehicle, some were not."

She leveled her gaze at Galleon and raised an eyebrow.

Galleon leaned back, nodded to her to continue.

"The attending doctors were wondering how, without any trauma to the head, he could have significant undiagnosed brain trauma and damage."

Galleon smiled at how Kaye had seemed to linger on the words *brain trauma*.

"I'll let our friend know," he said. "They've got to get him and put an end to this once and for all."

Chapter 19

Office of Technology and Research.

OTR.

Not *over the road* as Fenton's neighbor thought. Old Ray Buckner seemed like a pretty sharp senior citizen, but he was way off on that one. As soon as the old man uttered the acronym, Neagley knew it was a government organization and that Fenton was a man with secrets.

So she pulled the BMW down the street, drove until she found a park and fed Reacher his dinner. She only fed him high-quality food and she always had a handy collapsible rubber water bowl at the ready.

For herself, she had a travel mug of cold black coffee. It was all she needed. It had been the lifeblood of the Special Investigators.

While the dog ate, Neagley used her phone to

search the net for more information on OTR. She knew there wouldn't be much, but Wikipedia certainly ought to have the bare bones information, and it did.

The Office of Technology and Research was a division of the Department of Defense. Budget unknown. Personnel unknown. Stated mission: to develop new and innovative technology. *Ho-hum*, Neagley thought. If ever there was an umbrella statement to encapsulate basically anything under the sun, that was it.

What kind of technology? Offensive or defensive? Local or abroad? Financial technology? Military? Scientific?

Neagley racked her brain to think if she knew anyone who might be able to shed some light on OTR.

She came up blank.

She thought back to Fenton and the joint task force, how he had found the perp with computers, software and an algorithm. Of course, he would have wound up at OTR, and she had learned its headquarters were in a small town approximately halfway between Chicago and Rockford. That was just up the road and when Buckner had mentioned OTR, something had clicked for Neagley.

She took her time researching OTR. Using her phone for this kind of work wasn't her preferred method, but she was able to dig through her DOD databases and some information from the Pentagon. There wasn't much, but until she got back to her home office.

Now, Neagley got out of the car and put Reacher on a long leash—he was happily investigating every scent in the park. Neagley smirked. The real Reacher had been a pretty thorough investigator, too.

In the process of her research, Neagley remembered a man who'd been a computer forensic analyst and had briefly worked at the DOD. She found his email and sent him a note, asking if he could call her when he had a moment.

SHE SLIPPED the phone back inside her coat and waited until Reacher trotted back to the car, satisfied he'd covered every square inch of the park and had come up with nothing satisfactory.

Neagley put him into the back seat of the BMW, and then she slowly circled back to Fenton's house. She parked a block away, but the block opposite the neighbor she'd spoken with, and approached the house from the other direction. Instead of going around Fenton's house, she cut through the yard and entered his backyard from the other side, blocking her from view of Ray Buckner.

She'd already gotten a good look at the back door and knew the lock would be easy to pick. She also knew that the alarm, if there was one, would certainly have been disabled by the cops.

Of course, a lot might have been disabled by the cops, including any clues she might find. It was never terribly productive to investigate a crime scene that had already been processed and possibly compromised.

Neagley slid the lock-picking kit from her pocket and jimmied the lock within thirty seconds. She heard the mechanism click, and then the doorknob turned in her hand and she was inside, along with the dog. It was too cold to leave him in the car and she thought having a scent dog with her might be a good thing.

It was dark and she knew better than to turn on any kind of light, but a streetlight next door gave just enough illumination for her to make her way around.

Fenton's house was typical of a single male: comfortable furnishings, the minimum artwork, and a vague smell of man and fried food.

It was classic bungalow: dark wood, plaster walls, leaded glass windows. Wide open, roomy and comfortable.

Neagley knew the only room that would hold anything of value would be Fenton's office; she just had to find it. On the main floor was the kitchen, living room, dining room with built-in china cabinet, and a bathroom. Upstairs, she found a master bedroom and two smaller bedrooms.

The smallest of the bedrooms was dominated by one long desk and an empty space where computers would have been. That would have been taken by Chicago PD, most likely. If it hadn't been them, well, Neagley knew OTR would have come and cleaned out the computers.

The wastebasket was empty, and the wall was lined with bookshelves with books on computers and coding.

Neagley took the time to go through the bookshelves, riffle through the book pages and search for any hidden areas.

She came up with nothing.

Inside the master bedroom, she found an unmade bed and nothing else. The bathroom held the bare essentials. Toothbrush, shaving kit, deodorant and cologne. No odd prescriptions, no signs of illicit pharmaceuticals.

From downstairs, she heard Reacher bark.

It gave Neagley pause. Reacher was a fairly quiet dog, and if the bark was a warning, she'd heard no one approaching the house. Still, she didn't want to alarm the neighbors so she hurried downstairs as quickly as she could.

Reacher stood in the middle of the kitchen. At his feet was a plastic bag. Even from a distance, Neagley could smell it.

It was the unmistakable scent of dead fish.

Neagley went to the bag and carefully picked it up by its edge.

There was a piece of tape on the side and someone had handwritten the name Gulf Seafood Company.

The bag was empty, save for some foul-smelling liquid.

Neagley looked around the kitchen—where had the dog found it?

She walked into the living room and saw something else in the middle of the floor: a manila file folder. It too had a handwritten label with the name Gulf Seafood Company. It was empty, and she wondered if the plastic bag had been placed inside the manila folder. Maybe Reacher had dug it out.

She looked around the living room. Reacher walked in.

Neagley turned to him, held up the plastic bag and the folder.

Reacher cocked his head at her. His eyes were bright. *He almost looks proud of himself*, Neagley thought.

He then scratched at the living room rug, pulled up a corner.

There was a shallow, recessed cubby under the rug with a small brass ring.

Neagley smiled at her dog.

"Good boy," she said.

Chapter 20

Chavez lived in a two-story condo, with the first level being a garage. The main level consisted of a great room, kitchen, and sectioned off the central space, a long rectangular office that faced the ocean.

This was Chavez's office and the wall facing the ocean consisted of floor-to-ceiling windows. Hurricane proof, of course. The view was spectacular, although ninety-nine percent of the time, Chavez's eyes were glued to a computer screen.

Now, seated at his desk, he started up Thomas Greer's computer.

He'd already been through it but had not thoroughly perused every image and document in every folder. So when he'd gotten to the folder marked fish—and then the subfolders with grouper, snapper, snook, etc., he'd looked at the sample of photos in each: they all showed Thomas Greer holding up a fish he'd caught, whether it was in his official capacity or his hobby as a fisherman.

Chavez remembered that out of all of the folders, the one marked "shark" had consumed the most amount of computer memory, but he'd dismissed that fact because the area's waters were known as the shark tooth capital of the world, and plenty of sharks were to be caught as well.

At that time, he'd assumed the folder simply contained more of Greer's fishing prize photos.

But now, he opened the folder and sorted them by document type.

He ignored the JPEGs and instead focused on PDFs or Word documents. There were several that looked to be case files from the Florida Fish and Game Department, and soon Chavez zeroed in on a short document clearly written by Greer himself.

It involved an illegal shark fin harvesting operation.

When Avila had talked to Chavez about certain "delicacies" in foreign countries supposedly possessing special qualities, possibly sexual, the first thing Chavez had thought of was shark fin soup—considered by the Chinese to hold special sexual powers.

And just like that, he'd remembered the shark folder on Greer's computer.

What were the odds that Greer had been killed during a possible investigation into the illegal shark fin trade?

Now, he studied Greer's document. It was an early draft, perhaps written at home, out of the office, where he could concentrate on the first draft. And then later, at the office, he could polish and revise the document before submitting it to his superiors.

Even if it was an earlier draft of a document that Greer may have officially entered into the case files, it showed that he had begun becoming suspicious of a local outfit and their shark catches.

Chavez read it with growing interest until at the very end he saw the name of the company Greer was targeting: Gulf Seafood Company.

Chavez did an online search for the company and found absolutely nothing. How could that be? He had figured that there were probably multiple companies, restaurants or fishing operations with that name.

But his online search had come up blank.

The best way to find out more about this mysterious entity was to trace its financials and that was something Chavez could do, but he also knew someone who could do it much, much better and faster.

She was another one of Jack Reacher's Special Investigators. A savvy investigator with a brilliant mathematical and financial mind.

Karla Dixon.

Chapter 21

"Do you see the area of damage?"

Chicago Police Detective Alex Yates studied the X-ray. It showed a human brain covered with bright spots, like some kind of medical constellation. He was tempted to look for the Big Dipper.

Even though he wasn't an expert, Yates knew the spots were bad and it was fairly obvious the trauma was extensive. In fact, even after years of looking at various wounds via X-rays, he'd never seen a brain injury like it.

"Yes," he said. "Clearly. But I still don't understand."

They were in Fenton's hospital room at Chicago Central, with the attending physician, a woman named O'Connor, and her physician's assistant, Tilford. Dr. O'Connor was a tall woman with short blonde hair and stylish yellow glasses.

"How could he have all of this internal brain injury, without a scratch on his head?" Yates asked. "Whiplash?"

O'Connor shook her head. "Great question, but not likely. Whiplash is a very specific type of trauma and there's nothing here to indicate that kind of injury. But you're right, that's the very first thing we noticed. He had some mild internal injuries from the car accident, but luckily, the driver hit the brakes just before impact so nothing was broken. However, we ran a CAT scan just to be safe and we found this."

"Then what is it?"

"I once saw an Iraqi combat veteran with something vaguely similar," the doctor responded. "But please let me emphasize, it shared only a few characteristics, commonly caused by blast waves."

"As in, from bombs? Artillery?" Yates asked.

"Indeed," O'Connor said. "A blast wave is a result of the force of the bomb's dispersed energy and it can literally push the brain so hard it causes severe damage. Sometimes the effects of the damage don't show up right away until the patient exhibits certain types of behavior. Memory loss, confusion, anger and in some cases, violence."

"The most common injuries are concussion," Tilford added.

"A concussion is the mildest result," O'Connor explained. "Some injuries can be quite severe, certainly causing death. This case has a somewhat similar pattern, but it seems omnidirectional, which is very strange and, I must say, unique."

"Omnidirectional?" Yates asked. "You mean, like multiple bombs exploding all at once?"

"It's difficult to speculate," O'Connor replied. "A blast wave typically comes in a single direction and pushes the brain in that same direction with its force. In this case, it appears the wave was almost internal and the damage so pervasive, almost going outward. Like I said, I've never seen anything like it. In fact, I've asked several of my colleagues to weigh in on the injury. In particular, one physician I know who has vast experience with battlefield injuries. I should know more later today."

She turned toward the doorway as a hospital employee entered the room. The doctor was annoyed.

"Could you please wait–" she began.

The orderly ignored her. He had olive skin, jet-black hair and dark eyes.

Yates pegged him as Chinese, most likely. He was looking at the back of the room where Fenton lay in his hospital bed. Fenton's eyes were half-closed and Yates knew he'd been given some pain medication as well as a cocktail of chemicals to reduce his brain swelling and hopefully relieve some of the worst symptoms.

The Asian man moved toward Fenton and O'Connor objected.

"That's my patient," the doctor said. "Do not disturb–"

When the man slipped his hand inside his white lab coat, Yates knew something was horribly wrong.

The detective reached for his own gun and the room exploded with gunfire.

Chapter 22

Neagley poured herself a rare glass of wine and sat on the outdoor patio of her home, overlooking Lake Michigan. It was a grand view: a long sheet of frozen water, blanketed with snow, and the fading orange horizon in the distance.

It was cold, but only the beginning. It would get much colder. Even though the patio was heated, with terra cotta floor tile and enclosed with windows, the chill found its way in. In the depths of a Chicago winter, the place would not be pleasant to enjoy a glass of wine. So Neagley was savoring both the cabernet and the moment.

Her phone rang and she saw it was the friend she'd contacted about OTR.

His name was Reynolds.

"Hey," she said.

"I don't even want to know why you're asking about these guys," Reynolds said.

"Is it that bad?"

"Worse."

Neagley put down her wineglass. "Tell me."

Reynolds was more of an acquaintance than a friend, but they had worked together in the Army, and there was a certain amount of trust, to a point. As she recalled, he had asked her out a couple of times and she naturally had turned him down. But unlike some guys, Reynolds had taken it like a champ and they had ultimately forged a tentative friendship over the years. He was an intelligent guy and worked in logistics at the DOD. The perfect position to possibly provide insight on a little known section of the organization.

"Don't worry, this is confidential," Neagley said.

"That's just it, these guys would probably know anyway," Reynolds laughed.

"What do you mean? Like, they're NSA?" The National Security Agency was famous for the Patriot Act and its ability to eavesdrop on just about anyone at any time.

"Not really," Reynolds said. "Let's just say OTR is the place where the tools are developed to be used by NSA and others. They're like the cool kids with the latest gadgets or software or scientific research that are game changers. That's why they're so secretive and no one's ever heard of them. They don't actually do the dirty work, they just develop the stuff that allows others to do the job."

"I think I'd heard the name, but never really knew what they did."

"No one really does," Reynolds said. "In fact, most of what I'm telling you is rumor and gossip around DOD. I could be wrong, but OTR has the reputation as being one of the most dangerous and best kept secrets in the military. Why are you asking about them?"

"A guy I knew in the Army disappeared, and I think he worked, or works, at OTR."

"Yikes. Be careful, Neagley. When it comes to OTR, the people in charge play for keeps. There's a lot at stake, if you know what I mean."

She did know what he meant. It sounded like OTR was the kind of thing kept under wraps and if it was somehow revealed to the public, the publicity could make a whole host of dangerous people look bad. And there was nothing good about backing those kind of people into a corner. They had a way of making problems, and the people who cause them, disappear.

"Since technology is in the name, I'm assuming that's what this is all about. New types of weapons or something?" Neagley asked, a hint of skepticism in her voice.

Reynolds laughed. "Yeah, but you're forgetting the other half of their name: Research."

"I assumed it was technological research."

"I'm sure it is, but the rumors I heard was they use that word to encompass all kinds of stuff: chemical warfare, biological warfare, psychological methodologies—basically anything and everything that falls under applications that can have military value."

Neagley thought about that. She also wondered about Fenton and his disappearance. The witness who said his car was moved, the full tank of gas, and the man was still missing.

"Look, I have to run, but if you have any questions, don't call me again," Reynolds joked, but at the same time, Neagley knew he didn't want to talk much longer. "Kidding, of course. But I wouldn't be surprised if this kind of thing wouldn't go unnoticed. Did you contact anyone at OTR?"

"No."

"Good. Don't. You're better off without them in your life."

Neagley thanked Reynolds and hung up. She wasn't terribly surprised by what she'd learned but still had no way to tie it to why Fenton was missing and who might have wanted to make him go away.

The only lead she had was the plastic bag Reacher had found in Fenton's hiding spot.

It was time for another shortcut. She needed someone to find out who or what Gulf Seafood Company was, and what the hell it had to do with a secret government agency.

Neagley thought about people at her security firm who could do the job. But none of them would be as fast, insightful and thorough as Karla Dixon. The woman could dissect a company's financials in less time than it takes to grill a steak.

She dialed Dixon's phone number. Karla picked up right away and as usual, Neagley got right to the point.

"Did you say Gulf Seafood Company?" Dixon asked. Her voice sounded odd.

"Yes. Why?"

Dixon chuckled. "You're not going to believe this," she said.

Chapter 23

Henry Mah was a fastidious man. He was always well-groomed, often bathed twice a day and placed a premium on keeping things organized, which he believed made it infinitely easier to maintain optimum cleanliness.

To say he hated messes was an understatement.

Which is why he was boiling with rage over the chaos that erupted at Central Hospital. They'd finally located the pain in the ass James Fenton and moved to eliminate him once and for all.

Instead, they killed a Chicago detective, wounded three innocent hospital workers, and Mah lost both of his men assigned to the hit.

Two dead Chinese operatives that would soon come under the full scrutiny of the Chicago Police Department, in retaliation for their murdered man. But, even worse, possibly the FBI and should things escalate in the worst possible way, the CIA.

Now, clean up was all Mah had in mind.

It would all begin with that stupid man Galleon and his freaky assistant Kaye.

They had called him and told him they'd found the man he was looking for, but failed to inform him the local cops had already found him, too. Had he been set up? Mah didn't think so, but it wouldn't surprise him. Galleon was a slick Washington man, and the redhead Kaye was as cold as a month-old cadaver.

Mah despised the American intelligence community and Galleon in particular. Although the man had helped him infiltrate certain elements of the criminal community, there had been precious little value provided via the relationship.

HENRY MAH WAS no ordinary gangster. He was also a senior agent in China's Ministry of State Security. The MSS was his country's version of the CIA, MI6 and the KGB.

He had been tasked with consolidating rival Chinese criminal organizations, but that project had only been the first step on his assigned ladder.

The second phase of the operation had been going quite well until James Fenton had decided to expose some of the work Mah and his team had done.

In addition to a ruthlessness as pure as fire-hardened crystal and ambition in buckets, Henry Mah had one more important feature at his disposal: resources.

Lots and lots of resources courtesy of his home country's deep pockets.

What was at stake was much more than criminal territory, and even money. It was the balance of power thanks to an incredible technology that could change things forever not just for China, but for himself. He would be a national hero, perhaps known only to a few people behind closed doors. But those people were the most powerful individuals in China, and his work would not go unrewarded.

Mah sent out instructions through his intermediaries. It was time to take the velvet glove off the iron fist and teach the Americans how things were meant to be accomplished.

Although he had personally killed Avan Luu in order to complete phase one of the plan, he generally preferred to keep his hands clean, a nod to his well-known affinity for simplicity and sterility.

This, however, would be different.

He stood, went to the gun cabinet hidden

behind a bookcase in his personal office and chose a .45 automatic fitted with a silencer.

He took extra clips but figured he wouldn't need them. He had three targets of primary importance: Fenton, Galleon and that bitch Kaye.

Anyone who got in his way would be immediately added to the list, and eliminated.

Galleon and Kaye were his counterparts and they would no doubt die as heroes.

But they would die, nonetheless.

Chapter 24

While Frances Neagley had been the most like Jack Reacher in terms of propensity for violence and impressive physicality, Karla Dixon had been the special investigator who shared the most intellectual similarities with him.

In particular, their love of numbers, mathematics, equations as well as practical problems and solutions. They loved to challenge one another with number-based puzzles.

Dixon had always held her own and won more often than not.

She had a gift for figures and could rapidly complete complex calculations in her mind, like a chess player visualizing forty moves ahead.

After she left the Army, she took her skills to New York and soon earned a top position with a forensic accounting firm.

When she had begun working on Chavez's (and quickly afterward Neagley's) request for financial information on an outfit called Gulf Seafood Company, ostensibly based out of Venice, Florida, she had made it a top priority. *You do not mess with the special investigators.* Dixon smiled at the self-styled slogan they had all embraced.

The organization that had become Chavez's and Neagley's target would have filed papers with the state of Florida, and that's where Dixon began her search. Very quickly, Karla realized Gulf Seafood Company was a total fabrication.

The addresses provided were not legitimate, the phone numbers supplied were disconnected and the names listed on the corporate filings were traced to either dead individuals or people with no records whatsoever.

So, the company was a front.

Still, if there was actual business being done, even if it was illegitimate, that meant there were transfers of money. Although cash transactions were always difficult to trace, Dixon knew that if the same company had popped up on the radars of both Neagley and Chavez, this was not some tiny mom and pop operation hiding a few thousand dollars under the cash register.

So she dug.

The nice thing about numbers and banking was that to a certain degree, they have to be real.

Fake bank numbers would result in an inability to perform transactions. So Dixon searched for any and all actual banking information associated with Gulf Seafood Company.

Eventually, she found one: the company's initial filing fee in the state of Florida.

It was the first thread she would use to unravel what she intuitively reasoned was going to be a big heaping pile of bullshit.

Chapter 25

"You first," Neagley said.

Chavez laughed inwardly, *classic Neagley*, he thought. Right to business, no personal chit chat, catching up with each other, wasted words.

"Gulf Seafood Company," Chavez said. "A former client of mine's husband worked for Florida Fish & Game. He was murdered two days ago. No apparent motive, until I talked to his supervisor. Turns out they were investigating this Gulf Seafood Company for possibly being involved in the illegal shark fin trade. In particular, my client's husband had taken it on himself as a bit of a pet project, so to speak."

"What happened to him?"

"They gutted and skinned him in the swamp."

There was silence on the other end of the line until Neagley began speaking.

"A man named James Fenton disappeared a few days ago. I worked with him back in the day on a case involving a serial rapist, and Fenton came through big time. So when I heard about his disappearance, I decided to look into it. Turns out he is, or was, a computer and tech genius working for OTR – the Office of Technology and Research."

"I've vaguely heard of those guys."

"That's what everyone says. OTR is within the Department of Defense. Very secretive. Apparently they use the 'Research' part of their name to develop all kinds of things with weapons potential."

"Of course they do."

"Inside Fenton's house was a hidden compartment where I found an empty package with the name of the seafood company written on it. If it had been in the fridge or something, I might have overlooked it. But Fenton hid it for a reason. I'm guessing he wanted it as evidence of something. Proof. So I needed to find out more about this mystery fish company and I called Dixon, apparently not long after you had reached out to her."

"How the hell are a Florida Fish and Game officer and a computer nerd with OTR linked?" Chavez wondered.

"That's the big question," Neagley answered. "I've got a few theories."

"Let's hear 'em."

"In person, Chavez."

He chuckled. "You want me to fly up?"

"I think the bigger pieces of the puzzle are up here in Chicago, not down there."

"Okay."

"I've already booked your flight," Neagley replied. "You've got just under an hour to get to the airport. Don't take the freeway it looks like there's congestion. Take Highway 41 and you'll get there quicker."

Chavez was taken back to the Army and the special investigators. Neagley had been a machine back then, and some things never changed.

He started to thank her for making his arrangements, but she had already hung up.

Chapter 26

The noises were so loud he thought his head was going to explode. The pressure pulsed against the inside of his skull and he winced, cried out.

No one was listening.

All around him was chaos.

People screamed. There was blood on the floor and smoke in the air.

In the distance, he heard sirens. Fire alarms were going off and water was spraying down from the hospital room ceiling.

James Fenton swung his feet down from the hospital bed.

There were two men dead on the floor. Both were Asian. There was another dead man across the room and two women were slumped against the wall. They were covered in blood but he didn't know if they were dead or alive.

Fenton stood and the room swirled.

Was the hospital on fire?

Why was he in a hospital? He remembered running and then seeing a truck.

Now, he ran from the room.

There were others also running. It looked like they were going for the stairs.

He blended in with everyone else. He looked down, saw he was wearing glorified pajama bottoms. They were blue and felt almost like paper. A weird cotton shirt tied at the back. On his arm was a piece of tape and a tube flapping as he ran. He tore off the tube and threw it on the ground.

Panic clouded his mind.

All that remained in his consciousness was a series of numbers and a name.

811 McKenzie.

What the hell did it mean?

He had no idea. But it was almost like a detached voice yelling the number and name at him over and over again. It sounded like something that would make him feel safe. Maybe protect him.

There were more sirens and people shouting. A clog of people were negotiating their way down the stairwell, talking about active shooters and police and some people were crying, dialing their cell phones as they tried to run.

He came to a door packed with a crush of people and off to his right, another door. He darted to the second one and he pushed through it, finding himself in another short hallway. At the end was another door with people running out. He followed them and burst outside, into the cold.

The frigid air shot through his paper-thin clothing and he saw a person get into a yellow car. Behind that car was another yellow vehicle.

Fenton raced to it, opened the back door and jumped inside. It was warm, and smelled like cigarette smoke and whiskey.

The man behind the wheel looked at him, seemingly unperturbed by the rush of people or the sirens.

"811 McKenzie," Fenton said. It just popped out of his mouth, unbidden.

The driver put the car in gear. "You got it, buddy."

Chapter 27

"Where's Reacher?" Chavez asked.

His flight up from Florida had been uneventful and when he'd exited the terminal at O'Hare, he'd spotted Neagley perfectly positioned in her BMW to pick him up. The bitter Chicago cold was a shocking difference from warm and still muggy Florida.

But Chavez had a smile on his face. Word had gotten out among Jack Reacher's special investigators that Neagley had gotten a dog and named him Reacher.

It brought a lot of mirth and merriment to the team.

Chavez thought: *You do not mess with the special investigators, unless one of them gets a dog and names him Reacher.*

"He's at home," Neagley said.

"Is that where we're going?"

"Let's find out right now."

Neagley punched the speaker phone button and her car's Bluetooth came to life. She told it to call Karla Dixon.

Moments later, Dixon's voice came through the BMW's dozen speakers or so. Chavez wondered how good his favorite band – the Rolling Stones – and their music would sound coming through the big vehicle's sound system. Probably better than he'd ever heard them, and he'd seen them live in concert.

Twice.

Dixon's voice was so clear it sounded like she was sitting behind them speaking directly into their ears.

"Neagley," Dixon said.

"I'm here, too, Karla," Chavez chimed in.

"What did you find?" Neagley asked, preempting any small talk. Chavez imagined Dixon's expression in New York probably mirrored his own: slight amusement that Neagley hadn't changed one bit.

"Gulf Seafood Company is essentially a shell company whose real ownership is in China. I suspect it's a government entity, run out of Beijing. Typically, agents from their Ministry of State Security, MSS, are tasked with running the show."

"Your rationale?" Neagley asked.

"The company's setup is way too complicated to be run by, say, a Chinese triad in Florida. No way. Those guys aren't this sophisticated. Someone with some real brains and fairly deep pockets put this whole thing together."

"Why would the Chinese government or its intelligence organization want a seafood company in Florida? Just for access to illegally harvested shark fins?" Chavez asked.

"Two birds with one stone," Dixon replied. "Yes, they are certainly participating in the illegal shark fin trade. The files you found on Greer's computer provided a fairly clear picture of that. But that's just a side part of the main hustle. The reason for Gulf Seafood's existence is money laundering."

"Ah," Neagley said. "That makes sense."

"Yep," Dixon continued. "Nearly everything about the company is fake except the harvesting of shark fins, their transportation, and the money. Oh, it's routed all over the place, but eventually, everything, the fins and the cash, all end up in Beijing."

"Jesus," Chavez says. "And I thought Venice was a quiet little tourist town."

"Nothing like this happens in China without the government knowing about it. Which tells me it's unequivocally state sanctioned. Now, the question I have is, why did MSS need to launder the money in the first place? What were they using it for?"

"That's what I was wondering," Neagley said. "China's a rich country, especially at the top. Why are they messing around with a seafood company in Florida?"

"That's the key," Dixon said. "Except, it's not, why Florida? It's why the U.S.?"

Chavez slapped his hand on the BMW's dashboard. "Because they were using the money for something in the United States. What better way to fund an American-based operation than with an American company?"

"And somehow, that money was connected to OTR," Neagley reasoned. "But how? And why?"

"I believe you're both correct," Dixon said. "Everything went back to Beijing, but pure cash transactions simply aren't traceable. I believe a significant chunk of profit was kept in the U.S. and redistributed. If it went to OTR, or to someone affiliated with the agency, it would make perfect sense."

Chavez slid a razor-thin laptop from his travel bag. "So if Beijing or MSS is funding or buying something from OTR, what exactly would it be," he said. He gestured at his computer. "I'm sure they aren't buying laptops."

"I don't know, but I have a feeling James Fenton does," Neagley pointed out.

Chavez was furiously working the keyboard of his laptop.

"We're missing something," Dixon observed.

"Lots of pieces of the picture are still missing," Neagley said. "But I feel like we've started to put a frame around it."

"You should check out Michael Galleon," Dixon said.

Chavez's ears perked up. "Why is that name familiar?" he asked.

"He was mentioned in one of the financial transactions," Dixon said. "Buried in the fine print. He's DOD and I did a quick search. He's got an account in the Grand Caymans, which I find highly coincidental. I wasn't able to tie any money from China or Gulf Seafood Company to him, but I find it odd that a DOD employee mentioned in a phony business also has an account in the Caymans."

"Check this out," Chavez said. He was reading from his computer screen. "Michael Galleon was also mentioned in one of the notes from Thomas Greer's computer. Remember, Dixon, Greer was the fish and game officer murdered in Florida."

"There's your link," Dixon said.

"Here's a theory," Neagley posited. "What if this Galleon is a double agent working with MSS and maybe Fenton found out about it and was going to blow the whistle on him. Which is why either someone made Fenton disappear, or maybe…"

"Maybe Fenton staged his own suicide because he was worried Galleon and the MSS were after him," Chavez said.

"And if Galleon could have used OTR's resources…" Dixon suggested.

"Fenton would have been in big, big trouble," Neagley finished the thought. "But that raises another question. Why didn't he just go to the cops?"

"No idea," Dixon replied.

"It says here Michael Galleon was former CIA with lots of time spent overseas," Chavez was reading from his computer screen again.

"That could be how he knows Fenton," Neagley said. "If he does, which I'm assuming is the case. Although I hate to guess, it feels right."

No one filled the silence until Karla Dixon said, "You guys want me to keep going?"

"Not yet," Neagley answered.

Chavez glanced over at her. "Thanks Karla, you really blew the lid off this thing."

Neagley's lack of social graces was legendary among the special investigators but she seemed unfazed by Chavez taking the lead in offering thanks to Dixon.

Chavez knew Dixon wouldn't be offended,

that's just the way Neagley was, along with her discomfort at being touched. It was just who Frances Neagley was. And they all loved her just the way she was.

They disconnected from the call with Dixon and Chavez started to offer a theory when Neagley's Bluetooth came to life again.

"Hello?" she said.

"Miss Neagley?" To Chavez, the voice sounded like it belonged to an old man, which distracted him from the humor in hearing Neagley quaintly being referred to as *Miss*.

"Yes?" Neagley shot a glance over at Chavez. The corner of her mouth was turned up in what for her passed as being amused.

"This is Ray Buckner. Remember we talked? I'm Jim Fenton's neighbor and you said to call if I thought of anything else."

"Yes, of course," Neagley said. She sat forward in the driver's seat.

"Well, I didn't think of anything," Bucker said. "But I do see something."

"What's that?"

"Jim Fenton. He's standing right in front of me."

Chapter 28

"There's something wrong with him."

Neagley had sped back to Fenton's house in the BMW, simultaneously breaking multiple traffic laws. Twice, Chavez had offered hushed prayers for his and Neagley's safekeeping.

This amused her.

Now, after she asked Chavez to retrieve two black bags from the trunk of the BMW, they were face-to-face with Ray Buckner and James Fenton. In Neagley's opinion, Fenton hadn't changed much. He seemed smaller, his shoulders more shrunken, and the wispy hair he had left was very thin. He still looked elfin-like, if middle-aged elves were actually a thing.

"He showed up in a cab and I heard shouting," Bucker explained. "I went out there and the cab driver was about to knock Jimmy's head off because he didn't have any money. I paid the guy and same as you saw something was really wrong." The old man's blue eyes lifted toward Fenton.

"Who are you?" Fenton asked. His eyes were unfocused and his mouth hung open crookedly. He looked like a mental patient off his meds.

"My name's Neagley," she said. "We've met before. Let's go back to your house and have a conversation."

"*My* house?" Fenton asked.

Neagley glanced at Buckner. "I think you should go back inside. We're going to call the police and they'll probably have some questions for you. I'll take care of Jim."

The old man was clearly tired and happy to extricate himself from the situation. Neagley was also getting a bad feeling; having conducted surveillance many times herself, she had an instinct for when the reverse was true: she felt like she was being watched.

She remembered what her friend Reynolds had said about OTR. They know and hear pretty much everything they want to. Which meant they might not be alone for long.

Buckner went back into his home and closed and locked the front door.

Neagley took Fenton and Chavez back to Fenton's home and entered through the back door.

If Fenton recognized his own house, he didn't mention it. He stood in the middle of the kitchen, looking like an uncomfortable guest.

Chavez had put the black bags on the kitchen table and now Neagley opened them.

"Here," she said and handed Chavez a .45 auto. For herself, she slipped a 9mm into her waistband and pulled out a pump shotgun with a shortened barrel.

Fenton watched like the spectator he was.

Without having to tell him, Chavez moved to the front of the house while Neagley and Fenton stayed in the kitchen, which had a clear view of the back door.

Neagley pulled out her phone and dialed 911.

"My name is Frances Neagley and I am calling to report that I believe I've found a person who was listed as missing. His name is James Fenton and we are located at his residence." She gave the dispatcher the address.

Neagley listened and was about to answer a question from the dispatcher when a window at the rear of the house exploded and gunshots rang out. A shower of glass cascaded onto the kitchen's maple floor and Neagley pulled Fenton to her, taking cover away from the doorway.

She could feel Fenton shaking with fear and confusion. His skin was cold to the touch and she wondered if he was in shock.

Chavez appeared, grabbed Fenton, and brought him to the living room, where he stashed him behind a large leather couch. "Stay there," he told him.

From her vantage point, Neagley could see the edge of the living room, and Chavez, who was ready with his .45, should anyone try to breach the front door. Neagley tightened her grip on the shotgun.

What was it Reacher always said? *Get your retaliation in first.*

Yeah, she wasn't a big fan of waiting, either.

She spun on her heel and leveled the shotgun at the back door. Just as she was about to pull the trigger, gunfire erupted outside. Neagley paused. No bullets came her way, or toward Chavez.

Who was shooting outside? she thought.

No sirens, so it certainly wasn't the cops.

And then, a voice.

Female.

"James?"

Neagley was surprised, but she recovered quickly. "He's busy at the moment," she said. "Perhaps I could answer any questions you may have. At least, until the cops arrive which should be any moment now."

More silence.

Chavez still hadn't moved. Neagley thought she could hear Fenton crying.

"My name's Kaye," the woman called out. "We're the good guys. We work with James."

We?

Neagley knew Chavez instantly understood what she did: there were two of them, one taking the back and one taking the front. Chavez would be ready.

"She's telling the truth," a man's voice called from the front. "We just want to get James into protective custody. It seems there are some very bad people out there who want to hurt him. We're with the government. We can protect him. You and the Chicago cops can't."

Neagley smirked.

"We'll take our chances with Chicago PD. I never trusted you government types anyway," she said and then took a gamble. "I'm assuming you're Galleon?"

Silence.

"I'm unarmed," the female called out. "I'm coming in."

"I wouldn't do that," Neagley replied, her voice cool.

The door slowly opened and Neagley watched as the woman appeared. She was ghostly pale with red hair and a mouth so severe it looked like a stab wound.

The woman raised a black plastic box. It had a

pair of buttons at the top and a narrow piece of dark glass.

Neagley immediately thought of the word "research" in OTR.

"This is just my phone," the woman said. "I called 911 too." The woman's fingers had come to rest on the buttons and Neagley could see the whiteness in the knuckles increase. The woman was starting to squeeze.

Neagley fired the shotgun.

A 12-gauge shotgun loaded with double ought buckshot can do horrendous damage to the human body. Neagley saw firsthand a prime example.

The redhead's body was very nearly cut in half as a huge chunk of the woman's midsection was simply blown apart in a terrific shower of blood and flesh. What was left of the body sagged and folded then slumped to the ground.

Neagley stood over the body and thought of what Jack Reacher used to say: *lights out*.

From the front of the house, gunfire sounded and Neagley recognized her .45. Chavez was no doubt making short work of the redhead's partner. She raced from the kitchen, through the dining room and into the living room where she saw Chavez standing over the body of a dead man.

He was distinguished-looking, with a touch of

gray at his temples and he was dressed in a fashionably cut suit.

The two bullet holes in his forehead didn't complete the ensemble.

In his hand was a black plastic box. A twin of the one the woman had tried to use.

Fenton was peeking over the top of the couch.

Chavez pointed at the black box.

"That's no phone," he said.

Neagley nodded. "Not even close."

Sirens sounded in the distance and Chavez and Neagley carefully retraced their steps out the back door. They found four dead men in Fenton's driveway. All of them were Asian, and one of them was dressed in a cheap suit, but a flashy gold Rolex was on his wrist.

In the window next door, Neagley saw Ray Buckner's worried face.

She gave him a little wave.

He didn't wave back.

Chapter 29

THREE MONTHS LATER

"WE NICKNAMED IT BOMB-IN-A-BOX," Fenton said.

He was still pale, but his eyes were focused and his mouth didn't hang crookedly anymore. Three months of medical treatment had done wonders. The doctors had focused on reducing his brain's inflammation and afterward, created a strict protocol to heal the tissue. While he might never fully recover, James Fenton knew who he was and just as importantly, knew what he did for a living and why he'd faked his own suicide.

"Handheld, capable of producing blast waves equal to some pretty serious weaponry," he continued. "As I can attest, it can do some pretty extensive damage to the human brain and body."

They were in Fenton's hospital room. A man from the Department of Defense was seated in a chair next to Fenton. Neagley was surprised she had finally been granted access to see him. Chavez had flown back up from Florida to join her for the meeting. They both knew it would be the first and last time Fenton would ever be allowed to tell them about his role in the ordeal.

"So that little black plastic box is what the Chinese were bribing Galleon for?" Neagley asked.

Fenton glanced at the DOD official who shook his head.

"I don't think I can comment on that," Fenton said. "Let me just say that the Chinese knew about it, and its potential to revolutionize warfare and close quarters combat. So, it wouldn't surprise me if they'd gone out of their way to bribe anyone working on the project. And of course, if I'd found out about it, I certainly would have blown the whistle."

Fenton was telling them exactly what happened, but making it sound hypothetical.

"That's enough," the official said.

Chavez offered a snort of derision. "Oh, come on," he said. "Do you really think we're going to run to the media and try to sell a Chinese conspiracy?"

"No," the official said. "That's why we allowed you in here. But you have enough of the picture now."

Fenton ignored him which made Neagley like him even more. "I thought I would have whistleblower protection when I went to Galleon. But then someone was following me and no one came to talk to me. I decided to fake my disappearance but someone got a partial blast on me, I guess," he said.

Neagley and Chavez had already worked out that part.

"Fortunately, it worked against them," Fenton continued. "Because my thoughts were scrambled I didn't know who I was or where I was. It made all that much harder for them to find me. Luckily, you got involved and showed up at just the right time."

The official finally stood up and two more DOD personnel walked into the room. One of them was older than the others and bore the posture of a man in charge.

"As we said before, Miss Neagley and Mr. Chavez, we thank you for your help," he said. "We sincerely appreciate your agreement to keep this all on a need-to-know basis."

"What about Dorothy Greer?" Chavez asked.

"Her husband died because he, too, had tied Galleon to this whole scheme and Henry Mah's men killed him."

"She will be taken care of financially, and we'll try to tell her what we can as long as it doesn't jeopardize national security," the leader of the DOD group said. "Mr. Greer will be recognized for the true hero he was."

Chavez shrugged his shoulders. It wasn't enough, but it would have to do.

"Now I'm sure you've got a plane to catch, Mr. Chavez," one of the other men said. "In fact, I believe it starts boarding in less than two hours. And Miss Neagley—"

"Why?"

The voice came from behind one of the men, who stepped aside to reveal James Fenton peering intently at Neagley.

"Why did you help me?" he asked.

Neagley thought about her answer.

"Years ago, you helped put away a man who was hurting a lot of women. No one could find him, or figure out who he was. Until you did. When I saw you had disappeared, I figured you might need some help and I felt like you'd done more than enough to deserve it."

Fenton nodded.

When Neagley and Chavez left, no one said a word.

Chapter 30

"Sure you don't want to come back with me?" Chavez asked. Neagley was driving him back to the airport. Winter was nearly over, but it had a well-deserved reputation for wearing out its welcome and staying too long. "How can you deal with this cold all the time? Venice is beautiful. Seventy degrees, sunny and great beaches."

"Would I have to see you in a Speedo?" she asked him.

"You should be so lucky."

The miles flew by and they shared stories of their time in the Army working under Reacher, about past cases and what their respective futures might hold. By the time they got to the airport, Neagley was surprised to feel disappointed Chavez was leaving.

"One day, I'm sure we'll see Reacher again, don't you think?" Chavez asked.

"I wouldn't be so sure of that," she answered. "I always think when he walks away it's the last time I'll ever see him. One of these times, I'll be right."

Chavez didn't disagree. It was the truth, and they both knew it.

They said goodbye to one another – no hugs, of course – and Neagley exited the airport and pointed the big car back toward home where *her* Reacher was patiently waiting.

THE END

BUY THE NEXT BOOK IN THE SERIES!

NEVER FORGIVE, NEVER FORGET : BOOK 4 IN JACK REACHER'S SPECIAL INVESTIGATORS

A USA TODAY
BESTSELLING BOOK

Book One in The JACK REACHER Cases

CLICK HERE TO BUY NOW

An Award-Winning
Bestselling Mystery Series

Buy DEAD WOOD, the first John Rockne Mystery.

CLICK HERE TO BUY

"Fast-paced, engaging, original."
-*NYTimes bestselling author Thomas Perry*

About the Author

Dan Ames is a USA TODAY Bestselling Author, Amazon Kindle #1 bestseller, GoodReads Readers Choice finalist and winner of the Independent Book Award for Crime Fiction.

www.authordanames.com
dan@authordanames.com

Also by Dan Ames

THE JACK REACHER CASES

The JACK REACHER Cases #1 (A Hard Man To Forget)

The JACK REACHER Cases #2 (The Right Man For Revenge)

The JACK REACHER Cases #3 (A Man Made For Killing)

The JACK REACHER Cases #4 (The Last Man To Murder)

The JACK REACHER Cases #5 (The Man With No Mercy)

The JACK REACHER Cases #6 (A Man Out For Blood)

The JACK REACHER Cases #7 (A Man Beyond The Law)

The JACK REACHER Cases #8 (The Man Who Walks Away)

The JACK REACHER Cases (The Man Who Strikes Fear)

The JACK REACHER Cases (The Man Who Stands Tall)

The JACK REACHER Cases (The Man Who Works Alone)

The Jack Reacher Cases (A Man Built For Justice)

The JACK REACHER Cases #13 (A Man Born for Battle)

The JACK REACHER Cases #14 (The Perfect Man for Payback)

The JACK REACHER Cases #15 (The Man Whose Aim Is True)

The JACK REACHER Cases #16 (The Man Who Dies Here)

The JACK REACHER Cases #17 (The Man With Nothing To Lose)

The JACK REACHER Cases #18 (The Man Who Never Goes Back)

The JACK REACHER Cases #19 (The Man From The Shadows)

The JACK REACHER CASES #20 (The Man Behind The Gun)

JACK REACHER'S SPECIAL INVESTIGATORS

BOOK ONE: DEAD MEN WALKING

BOOK TWO: GAME OVER

BOOK THREE: LIGHTS OUT

BOOK FOUR: NEVER FORGIVE, NEVER FORGET

BOOK FIVE: HIT THEM FAST, HIT THEM HARD

BOOK SIX: FINISH THE FIGHT

THE JOHN ROCKNE MYSTERIES

DEAD WOOD (John Rockne Mystery #1)

HARD ROCK (John Rockne Mystery #2)

COLD JADE (John Rockne Mystery #3)

LONG SHOT (John Rockne Mystery #4)

EASY PREY (John Rockne Mystery #5)

BODY BLOW (John Rockne Mystery #6)

THE WADE CARVER THRILLERS

MOLLY (Wade Carver Thriller #1)

SUGAR (Wade Carver Thriller #2)

ANGEL (Wade Carver Thriller #3)

THE WALLACE MACK THRILLERS

THE KILLING LEAGUE (Wallace Mack Thriller #1)
THE MURDER STORE (Wallace Mack Thriller #2)
FINDERS KILLERS (Wallace Mack Thriller #3)

THE MARY COOPER MYSTERIES

DEATH BY SARCASM (Mary Cooper Mystery #1)

MURDER WITH SARCASTIC INTENT (Mary Cooper Mystery #2)

GROSS SARCASTIC HOMICIDE (Mary Cooper Mystery #3)

THE CIRCUIT RIDER (WESTERNS)

THE CIRCUIT RIDER (Circuit Rider #1)
KILLER'S DRAW (Circuit Rider #2)

THE RAY MITCHELL THRILLERS

THE RECRUITER

KILLING THE RAT

HEAD SHOT

STANDALONE THRILLERS:

KILLER GROOVE (Rockne & Cooper Mystery #1)

BEER MONEY (Burr Ashland Mystery #1)

TO FIND A MOUNTAIN (A WWII Thriller)

BOX SETS:

AMES TO KILL

GROSSE POINTE PULP

GROSSE POINTE PULP 2

TOTAL SARCASM

WALLACE MACK THRILLER COLLECTION

SHORT STORIES:

THE GARBAGE COLLECTOR
BULLET RIVER
SCHOOL GIRL
HANGING CURVE
SCALE OF JUSTICE

Free Books And More

Would you like a FREE copy of my story BULLET RIVER and the chance to win a free Kindle?

Then sign up for the DAN AMES BOOK CLUB:

For special offers and new releases, sign up here

BUY THE NEXT BOOK IN THE SERIES!

CLICK HERE TO BUY

A USA TODAY
BESTSELLING BOOK

Book One in The JACK REACHER Cases

CLICK HERE TO BUY NOW

An Award-Winning
Bestselling Mystery Series

Buy DEAD WOOD, the first John Rockne Mystery.

CLICK HERE TO BUY

"Fast-paced, engaging, original."
-*NYTimes bestselling author Thomas Perry*

Also by Dan Ames

The JACK REACHER Cases #1 (A Hard Man To Forget)

The JACK REACHER Cases #2 (The Right Man For Revenge)

The JACK REACHER Cases #3 (A Man Made For Killing)

The JACK REACHER Cases #4 (The Last Man To Murder)

The JACK REACHER Cases #5 (The Man With No Mercy)

The JACK REACHER Cases #6 (A Man Out For Blood)

The Jack Reacher Cases #7 (A Man Beyond The Law)

The JACK REACHER Cases #8 (The Man Who Walks Away)

The JACK REACHER Cases (The Man Who Strikes Fear)

The JACK REACHER Cases (The Man Who Stands Tall)

The JACK REACHER Cases (The Man Who Works Alone)

The Jack Reacher Cases (A Man Built For Justice)

The JACK REACHER Cases #13 (A Man Born for

Battle)

The JACK REACHER Cases #14 (The Perfect Man for Payback)

The JACK REACHER Cases #15 (The Man Whose Aim Is True)

DEAD WOOD (John Rockne Mystery #1)

HARD ROCK (John Rockne Mystery #2)

COLD JADE (John Rockne Mystery #3)

LONG SHOT (John Rockne Mystery #4)

EASY PREY (John Rockne Mystery #5)

BODY BLOW (John Rockne Mystery #6)

MOLLY (Wade Carver Thriller #1)

SUGAR (Wade Carver Thriller #2)

ANGEL (Wade Carver Thriller #3)

THE KILLING LEAGUE (Wallace Mack Thriller #1)

THE MURDER STORE (Wallace Mack Thriller #2)

FINDERS KILLERS (Wallace Mack Thriller #3)

DEATH BY SARCASM (Mary Cooper Mystery #1)

MURDER WITH SARCASTIC INTENT (Mary Cooper Mystery #2)

GROSS SARCASTIC HOMICIDE (Mary Cooper Mystery #3)

KILLER GROOVE (Rockne & Cooper Mystery #1)

BEER MONEY (Burr Ashland Mystery #1)

THE CIRCUIT RIDER (Circuit Rider #1)
KILLER'S DRAW (Circuit Rider #2)

TO FIND A MOUNTAIN (A WWII Thriller)

STANDALONE THRILLERS:

THE RECRUITER
KILLING THE RAT
HEAD SHOT
THE BUTCHER

BOX SETS:

AMES TO KILL
GROSSE POINTE PULP
GROSSE POINTE PULP 2
TOTAL SARCASM
WALLACE MACK THRILLER COLLECTION

SHORT STORIES:

THE GARBAGE COLLECTOR

BULLET RIVER
SCHOOL GIRL
HANGING CURVE
SCALE OF JUSTICE

About the Author

Dan Ames is a USA TODAY Bestselling Author, Amazon Kindle #1 bestseller, GoodReads Readers Choice finalist and winner of the Independent Book Award for Crime Fiction.

www.authordanames.com
dan@authordanames.com

Free Books And More

**Would you like a FREE copy
of my story BULLET RIVER and the
chance
to win a free Kindle?**

**Then sign up for the DAN AMES BOOK
CLUB:**

For special offers and new releases, sign up here

Printed in Great Britain
by Amazon